Candidate

Everyone

Joseph Cox

Published by Big Picture Books

Modiin, Israel

Cover Photo by Lucas Sankey on Unsplash

Edited by Wouter Dreyer

Feedback from many friends & associates – you know who you are!

Dedicated to Everyone :)

Coffee

By the third cup of coffee, I knew I had him hooked.

I'd moved to D.C. three years earlier. I'd come here because I wanted to be in on the center of the action. I could have gotten along fine living out in the middle of nowhere (in the 'provinces,' as I'd started to call them). I could have grown old not mattering. Or... I could make a stab at being in the place where it seemed like everything important in *your* life got decided.

For me, the choice was obvious.

But just being in the place wasn't enough. I didn't want to be a nobody whose only connection to power was that I cleaned power's offices. I wanted more. I wanted to really matter. And that, of course, wasn't easy.

The obvious way to get in, to matter, was to get elected. Those were the big boys in town. But getting elected takes time. Serious time. You can't (generally) just skip and jump into the House of Representatives, much less the Senate. You have to put your time in on the City Council, state legislature etc... etc... etc... I didn't have the patience. To be honest, I probably didn't have the charisma to pull it off, even if I had had the patience. So that was a no go.

The next option was to get on somebody's staff. Sometimes the staff matters more than the face on the front of the office. But that wasn't going to work for me either. Those folks, the ones who mattered, fell into two broad categories. The first group came from hoity-toity Ivy League schools with all the right connections. They were operators. The second group were those interns who specialized in 'extracurricular' skills. I would have been up for that, I think. But, quite brutally, I don't have the looks to compensate for my weight. I'm the kind of woman whose most likely to reproduce thanks to the anonymous services of a sperm bank.

There was another path, a classic path. Get involved in a campaign. Volunteer. Get close to the candidate and then get in on some cushy job. Of course, that was really just the same as getting elected. To be really close to the candidate you had to come up through the ranks with them. Otherwise, you were likely as not to be tossed aside once the election was won (or more likely, lost). And if you didn't pick the right candidate, you wouldn't go anywhere.

And so, I did the only thing that made sense to me. After I graduated college with a useless degree in theater, I imitated aspiring actresses everywhere. I said goodbye to my parents in Minneapolis, grabbed my dog, hopped into my crappy old gray Honda Civic and just drove to D.C. I got a job as a barista. And because it didn't pay much, I lived in that Civic. Then, I just kind of hoped for the best.

Up until that day, it hadn't exactly been working out.

It actually hadn't been working out for years.

And then *he* came into the coffee shop. I could see, right away, that he was an operator. He had the eyes of a man on the make. He had what my daddy used to call a "sh-t eating grin" on his face. And he looked like he was in a seriously good mood. But one thing he didn't look like was a socially conscious individual. And that was weird. Because the coffee shop wasn't exactly normal. I mean, normal people didn't go there. We took the whole personalized small batch, fair trade, farm to cup yada yada yada thing to a crazy extreme. The founder actually sourced each batch of beans from individual *family* plantations (none of this industrial scale stuff for us) and then tracked

8

it through every stage of its life – until it ended up in your cup. This stuff was crazy expensive and, in my opinion at least, not very good.

But... the people who came here were sending a message. They wanted other people to know they were socially aware. And we catered to that. Barely tolerable 'world music' was piped through the speakers (we picked it because it was barely tolerable, a little sacrifice can make people feel particularly virtuous). The walls were paneled with rustic-looking bamboo (sourced at Home Depot). And plants seemed to hang from every available space. While they created a maintenance headache, our patrons could argue they'd been Forest Bathing with their coffee. Our customers wanted to feel good about themselves. And when they came into our shop, they did.

But this guy already felt good about himself.

So good, in fact, that he didn't notice his coffee was $12 a cup. But I knew he could afford it. His clothes were not only impeccable, they were seriously stylish. Too stylish for D.C., in fact. After all, you don't want to *look* like an operator, even if you are - the constituents might get suspicious.

When the shop first started up, the coffee wasn't $12 a cup. Nobody would pay that much. The founder got himself into serious financial trouble. He had this vision and he spent a crazy amount of money setting up his sourcing and his tracing. And there was no way it could pencil out. Even if he sold a $5 coffee every 30 seconds, he wouldn't be able to pay off his investment.

And then I showed up.

He hired me as a barista. I think he did it because, *because* I was hideous and from the middle of nowhere. I fit the socially conscious image. But he got more than a barista when he took me on; I might not be book smart or beautiful, but I am incredibly good at getting things done.

And I knew, as soon as I realized what troubles he was having, just what he needed to do.

That day, when that stylishly dressed customer came in, I thought about asking him which family coffee plantation he wanted his brew from. But that might have killed his buzz. So instead, I just chose for him. And then, I made his cup, delivered it to him, and pointed out the little barcode I'd just printed on it.

"What's that?" he asked, perhaps more open than he'd have been on a normal day.

"Just scan it, watch and let me know what you think."

And so, he did. He took the coffee to a table, scanned the little barcode and started watching.

I actually saw him silently mouth a massive "Holy S---" as the video unfolded on his phone.

It was an even better reaction than I was hoping for.

You see, back when the founder of that little coffee shop was struggling, I knew he needed something really unique to *show* what his product was about. And so, I delivered it. It took a little work to convince him to pour more money into the venture, but he did. He paid for some camera equipment, he paid for a bunch of travel and he sent me to all of his little family coffee plantations. While there, I interviewed the family farmers. I talked to them about why they did what they did – from planting and picking to drying. I talked to them about why they were proud of the product they delivered. I talked to them about their heritage.

One thing about me: I might not be charismatic or beautiful, but people love to talk to me.

And then I flew to the millers, who hull, polish and sort the beans. And I did the same thing. And then I visited the exporters, who arranged the shipments of beans to our little store. And then I spoke to the roasters. And, finally, I interviewed all of our baristas. Afterwards, I put it all together, uniquely, for each cup. When a barista prepared your cup, a computer would assemble its history and then print the appropriate bar code on the side of it. When you scanned the barcode, you'd watch the story of *your* coffee. You'd meet the people involved every step of the way – even your barista.

And you'd know that your cup of coffee was more than just an average cuppa Joe.

That day, my stylish customer watched the video. And then he bought a second cup of coffee and watched another video. And then I saw him decide to buy a third.

And I *knew*, right then, that whatever he was up to I'd be in on it.

He wouldn't be able to resist.

When he came up to the counter, he asked the question I was waiting for. "Who made these?"

I just smiled at him, raised my hand, and said "me."

"No, no," he said, "Not the coffee, the videos."

"Me," I repeated.

He looked at me, not quite understanding.

And then it dawned on him that I meant exactly what I was saying.

Slowly, deliberately, he laid $12 on the counter, looked me in the eye, and said, "How'd you like a job?"

Those five words changed my life forever.
Actually, those five words changed *your* life too.

The Show

I knew I wanted to work for him, whatever the job was. But I couldn't make it that easy.

"What's the job?" I asked.

"Where did you go to film school?" he said. As if he hadn't heard me.

"I didn't," I answered.

He looked surprised.

"But the videos…"

"I figured out what this café needed and I taught myself," I said.

He just looked at me. And then a moment later I watched him emit a second, "Holy S---."

I just waited.

His grin broke for a moment. That was when he asked, with a tinge of actual desperation, "So, you just figure stuff out and get it done?"

"Yeah," I said.

And then he smiled, not the shit-eating-grin-I'm-good type of smile but the fine-Lordy-Lordy-just-saved-my-bacon type of smile.

"What?" I asked.

"Well," he said, "*I* don't just figure stuff out and get it done. I've got a very limited skill set. I'm kind of a sell *your* momma an ugly baby kind of guy. No offense intended"

"None taken."

"Yeah, well, a few months ago I had a really good idea. It doesn't happen much. But this one was a doozy. And so, I had to go with it. And I did. And I've sold it, in a way. But I'm more than a little worried I'm not going to be able to ride this particular horse."

"What was your idea?"

"Well, I set up two meetings today. One was with Senator William Kyle-"

"The politician? Who's considering running for President on the Democratic ticket?"

"The one. And the other was with Governor Jennifer Blumen, who happens to be in town."

"The front-runner on the Republican ticket."

He nodded.

"And they bought what you were selling?"

"Oh, yes."

"And it wasn't ugly babies."

"Nope."

"So, what was it?" I asked.

"An update." the man answered.

I just waited. He seemed a bit reluctant to spill the beans.

"Do you watch the debates?" he said.

"No," I answered.

"But you care about politics?"

"I want to be important, that's why I'm in D.C."

"What's wrong with the debates?"

"It's just a few people arguing, trying to score memorable points for their partisans. Two minutes and some web browsing can tell you all you need to know."

"Good, good," said the man. "In fact, ratings for debates having been declining with every election. If they aren't, they should be. So, I had an idea for something new. Instead of moribund old debates which really don't tell you anything about how candidates would do their jobs in the real world, I created something new."

"Which is?" I asked, my patience beginning to run a little thin.

"A series of challenges," said the man, "The candidates would compete in realistic situations. The public would judge their responses to complex problems. And then they'd vote, in rounds. Instead of a boring old debate we'd have something more fitting for today's world. And it would all be broadcast on the web."

"A reality show," I said.

He winced, but it wasn't for real. "I try to avoid that word, but yes. Today's candidates are reality show candidates, we should put them through their proper paces."

"Cool," I said. I was genuinely impressed. "And you sold this to Kyle and Blumen?"

"I did," he said, his grin returning. "They agreed, in writing, to participate in the contest."

"Wow."

"Yeah, but I'm afraid I can't deliver."

"Why not?"

"Well, I told them all about my production company, but there's nothing really there. I do have entertainment industry relationships, but they'll just take the whole idea from me. I can't keep control of it. And the financial backers? I could get them, but it'd be the same story. I'm not the kind of person who can manage it all."

"So, you need a manager."

"Yeah."

"A barista?" I asked, incredulous.

"Yeah, I think so."

"What makes you think I'm qualified?"

"The videos are *awesome*."

"That's it?" I asked.

"That and your general air of confidence."

"And why wouldn't I just take the idea from you, like your entertainment friends."

The man snorted.

"Look at you," he said, "You're smart, capable, driven. But you're a barista. Why? Because you can't sell yourself. So, you need me. I can sell anything. And I need you, because I can't deliver."

I looked him over. The man was a prick. But this was D.C. That was expected. And he wasn't wrong.

"Producer," I said.

"What?" he asked.

"I get to be called Producer. And I get 20% of the company. And I can manage whatever the heck I feel like."

He thought for just a second.

Then he grinned and extended his hand.

"I'm Freddie Samuels, and you've got a deal."

I took Freddie's hand.

"I'm Amber Martin and I'm in."

The Setup

The most important thing is for people to think you respect them. It doesn't actually have to be true to be effective. Sometimes, though, you really do respect people. And those people can come from the most unexpected places. To give one life-changing example: you might just find that kind of person is a barista at an incredibly snobby coffee shop.

Of course, I knew Amber was different from the moment I walked in. Not different in a good way, of course. She just didn't belong in that coffee shop; and I'm an expert on where people belong.

The kind of person who works there would have been vegan thin, and would have had a fair number of piercings, a couple of tattoos, long hair, and (dare I say it) a lack of personal hygiene. One thing Amber wasn't was vegan thin. She was 5-foot-nothing and 250 pounds. She could have eaten a vegan for breakfast and nobody would have noticed. Her jowls had jowls. She had no piercings and no tattoos. Her hair was thinning so much it seemed to have been falling out. She wasn't a fit in the personal hygiene department either; but in this case, the less said the better. I wouldn't have been surprised to see her selling deep-fried Snickers wrapped in chicken at a state fair. Except, of course, I'd never be at a state fair; unless it was to show respect to the kind of people who would be. I can be 'down home' if the circumstances call for it.

People and places fit together. Amber and that coffee shop didn't.

It so happened that at that exact moment in time, I didn't particularly care. I had just had the most successful day of my life.

I'd managed, in one day, to finagle meetings with two of the most prominent politicians in D.C. And I'd managed to sell them both. Sometimes a network can yield incredible benefits. As I said, the important thing is for people to think you respect them.

In either case, I'd had such an incredible day that I didn't mind buying a $12 coffee that tasted like native people had passed it personally because they'd run out of civet cats. I did notice the videos though. And after talking her up (and gently putting myself down), I managed to hire Amber on the spot. In reality, we became partners. I respected her abilities, she respected mine, and we worked extremely well together.

Our cadence was simple. I had the network and the face and she got the work done behind the scenes. And it all went very very well. We went from program planning in my dining room to pitching investors in glass and steel skyscrapers. Well, she prepared the material and I went to the pitches. We went from planning a purely online format to network television. Before long, she'd actually moved out of that disgusting car of hers and she began to smell like something that hadn't recently died.

That also helped with business.

And it was going to be an incredible business.

To make it that way we needed to dial things in perfectly. We needed a show people wanted to watch, but also a show they felt a little guilty actually turning on. Those pleasures are often the most undeniable.

In order to do this, we packaged the whole thing up as the next step in the grand American Democratic Experiment. We told the public our format would truly expose the candidates. Instead of

18

judging them by soundbites and snappy comebacks, we'd actually have some idea about how they'd perform under pressure.

It was all bullsh-t of course. But everybody knew that. They wouldn't have felt guilty if they didn't.

When we got brave enough, we even took it up a notch. I claimed, with a perfectly straight face, that our show would change the role of money in politics. Even as we planned to roll in the dough, we declared that we'd take the money out of politics. After all, everybody who made it to the show would have an equal chance. No amount of ad buying would be able to have more impact than their performance on our stage. The little guy would have as big a chance as the corporate or union-backed big guns.

This was a little closer to the truth, but not much. But people believe what they want to.

The most important thing, of course, was to make them want to *believe. Which is why I was the host. I would respect them (or at least appear to), and they'd buy whatever story I was selling. They'd think I had their interests at heart. That's why, when I said we'd take the money out of politics; they didn't really notice the obscene margins we were going to be making selling phenomenally expensive ads to politicians during the breaks.*

The show itself had to harness voters' passion. This started with selecting the candidates. We didn't have some fancy polling method. Instead, we went with an online poll. Voters could vote once a day for whomever they wanted. If they really liked somebody, they could vote for them day after day. If they were more sophisticated than the average bear, their dead relatives from Chicago could join in.

The idea was simple: we wanted committed, crazy, candidate support. With that would come buzz, conversation, ratings and... money.

*Once the candidates were selected, we couldn't run the actual voting. It just wasn't practical. We did the next best thing instead. We scheduled the show around the primaries with the final two candidates facing off just before the general election. It was simpler all around and we could still build up all the tension we wanted. We scheduled an episode to land before each major batch of primaries. And then the states ended up helping out from their end. Many of them shifted their primaries to match **our** timing.*

Before long, we were winding down to the final week before the primaries. The field of 16 was close to being announced. Everything was ready to go. The candidates were even sparring over the show itself. Before a single episode had been aired, they were complaining about bias and exclusion. The public was trying to work out my political views (hint, I don't have any). Everybody was playing every angle they could and no show in history had generated more buzz than ours.

It was perfect.

Then, two prominent candidates, withdrew. They made big public announcements – declaring the whole thing 'not Presidential.' They attacked everything we were doing.

*And that was **not** perfect.*

Amber actually considered just picking #17 and #18 to join the field. But let me ask you: how much do you actually know about the 17th and 18th most popular Presidential candidates? Not much, right. I knew we needed another solution to the problem. I just didn't know what it was. I still hadn't figured out what that replacement would be when I was invited to an interview on national TV. Any publicity is good publicity, so I accepted.

Once I was on the show, the host put two questions to me. First: "What do you think about the most prominent candidates backing out?"

That was an easy question to answer. I just had to throw aspersions on some unknown 'them'. I answered, "They're in the pockets of their Big Money donors, trying to give them one last chance to decide our elections." It was awesome populist pap.

And then she (the host) asked the big question: "What are you going to do about it?"

I didn't have an answer. Instead, I just announced that our staff had identified two candidates of our own. Dark horse candidates. Candidates of the people. We'd share them with the world the night of the show itself. I had no idea who those candidates were, of course. But social media went nuts with speculation. As I was driven back to the office, I imagined that all 5 feet and 250 pounds of Amber were scrambling through lists of no-name mayors and congressmen, trying to find a match.

It was an entertaining thought, and not far from the reality.

When I finally got there, I opened the door and Amber was standing there.

She basically shouted at me, "Who in the hell do you have in mind?"

I just smiled and said, "Amber, remember, it's all about the ratings."

She knew exactly what I meant. More than I did, in fact.

Amber called up the agent for the most popular reality TV star there was; a woman famous for her unusual fashion sense and outlandish ideas. She accepted our deal. Amber followed it up with another stroke of genius. She mapped the birth places of the other 15 candidates and then she picked the geographic point on the Continental U.S. that had the greatest average distance from all of them. We got a phone number, made a call – and offered the woman who answered the 16th spot.

It was incredibly effective. We introduced the candidates one by one. I was a charming, welcoming and positive host. Most of all, I was respectful. We were almost entirely non-partisan; you've got to treat the product well, right? Of course, in less obvious ways, I was just a bit more supportive of the candidate *I* wanted to win. Even if people had realized what I was doing, they wouldn't have known why. I wasn't actually a supporter of 'the man'.

Of course, we held back our mystery candidates until the very end. The anticipation was incredible. What had been a social media phenomenon became a hurricane. The reality show star had a short introduction – I explained that we chose her simply because of her remarkable popularity. Twitter exploded in speculation. And then she delivered her Statement – two minutes of pure political inanity. I just let her say whatever she wanted. I encouraged her to say whatever she wanted.

It was nuts. It was silly. But it made the real talent, the mainstream candidates, look great.

It gave them respect, and, folks loved it.

Nobody knew who the last candidate would be. Nobody but us. I rolled it out slowly. We (really Amber) made a splashy segment about how we found the last candidate – maps and lines and everything. The precise coordinate methodology necessary to find the perfect 16th candidate. We wanted to represent the *unrepresented. We wanted to give those without a voice a real voice. After a proper build-up, Charlotte Morris, a 63-year-old mother of three, was introduced. We'd coached her (as much as you can in a week) and helped her craft her statement. She was cogent, clear and a full-on nut-case conspiracy-theory right-winger. She did not display her respect of people across the political spectrum.*

Because of that she was an instant, and infamous, celebrity.

The rest of the campaign went beautifully.

*I wouldn't say it to her, of course, but Amber was perfect. Not only was she talented and gifted (which I **would** tell her), her incredible weight and sheer ugliness made her the perfect partner. She wasn't a threat to me. She couldn't replace me as host (obviously). And nobody was going to honeypot her into betraying me. There are limits to what people will do. We had trust and we had mutual interest.*

She was the perfect tool and I was the perfect opportunity.

The campaign itself went wonderfully. The two candidates who bowed out never stood a chance. The housewife offended 80% of the country, collected a few million votes and locked in a lifetime of talk-show income. The reality star made it into the second round. The world was abuzz with our project. And, in the end, a candidate hated by 50% of the population won the whole thing.

We called the show 'Choose your Leader'. It suggested that America would be choosing the next President. It suggested respect.

But in the end, the man I wanted won. He won precisely because I knew he'd alienate half of America.

I don't really respect the people.

But if you want something from them, you have to make them think you're the only one who does.

My Kind of Party

We had an employee watch party the night of the election itself. Our jobs were done. Now it was time to just sit back and enjoy the final results of our efforts. It is amazing how many people are needed in this sort of production, but between friends and family, no fewer than 3,000 people came to our event. We held it in a massive ballroom with thick red carpets, gold light fixtures and heavy drapery covering actual windows that overlooked Pennsylvania Ave. It had the glitz and glamour you can conjure when you've got the money. And I just sat there, watching the crowd, as waves of conversation flowed over me. This was the sound of success.

The evening was great. We really didn't care who won, we knew *we* were the winners. And that wasn't some losing candidate's conciliation speech. That was the simple truth. We had rocked the world and we were in a perfect position to do it again.

By that point, Freddie and I had been working together for two years. Together, we'd built the whole thing. I'd hired almost everybody in that room (well, not the friends and family). I'd managed them. I knew them. And, I suppose, I loved them. I'd gotten through hurdle after hurdle and deadline after deadline. And Freddie was the reason why. He'd not only created the concept; he'd made the whole thing pop. He got up there, wherever there was, and *everybody* was behind him.

Everybody loved Freddie.

As the party progressed, the number of people slowly diminished. Once the results were announced and the conciliation speeches made, there was a near rush for the doors. By 5am, everybody was gone. Even the cleaning crew had done their job. The smell of dawn, of a new and as yet empty day, filled the room.

I was about to head out to my trusty old Civic (I'd kept it, despite the money) when Freddie pulled me aside. He took me to a corner of the room – a space muted by the carpets and the drapery – put his hand on my shoulder, and asked "Amber, you know what comes next?"

I had no idea. As far as I could tell I was about to embark on a two-year vacation. You can't plan relevant challenges for a political reality show two years in advance. You can't even pick the candidates. Maybe he wanted miniature franchise versions for House and Senate races.

"No," I said, "I have no idea."

"It's obvious," he said, "Isn't it? Next time, *I* run for President."

I just stared at him and two thoughts ran through my head.

The first was, "He could win it."

The second was, "He really shouldn't."

I ditched both of them and asked, "Which party would you run with?"

He just looked at me with that crazy smile and said, "I don't need one."

It only took a moment, but then I realized he was right. He had created a new platform, a platform where he could succeed. And that scared me, just a bit.

"Listen," I said, "I'm very impressed with you. I'm impressed with your vision and with your ideas. But I don't think you have what a President should have?"

"And what's that?" he asked.

"Uh, I dunno... any sort of administrative capability!"

"I don't need that. I've got you."

That was smooth.

"Okay, then, how about policies?!?"

"You tell me, what *policies* are going to sew this country back together."

I couldn't think of any.

He pressed on. "So, do you really think I need policies?"

"What can you do without policy?"

"Classic horse trading," he said, "I give a little here, get a little there. I keep myself on top by managing the factions below. But that isn't policy. That's just a political balancing act and I think I'd be pretty good at it."

"So, no ideological allies?"

"I'll let everybody think I'm their ally. You know the story of Libya, right?"

I didn't really.

"I'll tell you then. A horrible dictator, Muammar Gaddafi – a guy who had grand and airheaded ideas floating out of his vapid head and on to the pages of his 'green book' – ran the place for decades. Everybody hated him. But they weren't killing each other. Then the U.S. helps him get killed. And guess what?"

"What?"

"The place went to sh-t. Everybody started killing everybody else. Everything he'd balanced together fell apart."

"So, you're Muammar Gaddafi?"

"No, but I'm related. This place is falling apart. We've got blackshirts. We've got domestic terrorists. Everybody is at everybody else's throats. It needs to settle down. It doesn't need policies – not enough people would ever be satisfied by policies. It needs balance and tradeoffs and de-escalation. Honestly, it needs somebody who wants power enough to make everybody just barely happy enough to stop going nuts. It doesn't need an ideologue. What it needs is me."

He had a point. It made quite a bit of sense.

He kept going.

"People fall into this opinion that a good leader is smart or intelligent or wise. But that's hogwash. Great leaders are *often* stupid. Wise people often think they know what's best. When they push for it, it often leads to conflict or even war. When people look at reality, they make it fit into whatever story makes them happy. If they think the economy should be booming, it is. If a really smart guy is forcing change that isn't in line with their values, they'll find every fault there is to find. But if an agreeable clown is in charge, somebody they think is on their team, then they'll see the best reality they can see."

"So, people just need some friendly guy they want to see the good in?"

"Exactly."

"And you want to be that dunce?"

"That's right. I'd be great for the job. I have no baggage and no history. I've treated every side fairly. People like me. The country is falling apart. So... they need me as their next President."

It was 5am, I was exhausted after the campaign, but he was making a surprising amount of sense.

A suspicion crept into my mind. The whole reality show created this opportunity. I had to ask, "Freddie... did you plan this from the very beginning?"

He just smiled. "You can't *plan* this sort of opportunity. But... perhaps... I dreamed of it."

His grin was huge.

"So, what's next?" I asked.

"Ah," he said, "That's what *you* have to tell me."

With that, he clapped me once on the shoulder, turned around and left. I stood in the empty hall.

I knew what was next. Freddie got us in the door, I put together our proposals and packages and plans and then Freddie closed the deal, whatever the deal was.

He was my opportunity and I was his tool.

And the sky was the limit.

The Plan

The first priority was publicity. Freddie's face needed to be everywhere; even though *Choose your Leader* wasn't on. He didn't need to be everywhere from day one. The occasional talk show could suffice, for now. After all, he was an acknowledged political guru now, he could get those appearances easily enough.

But he would need more. He would need something to get him in front of the eyes of people who weren't just political wonks. He couldn't start his own talk show. That would force him to start talking policy and we both agreed that wouldn't be a good idea.

Somehow, he needed to get his months in the sun. He needed a show, but one that didn't demand any policy positions. Without that, he'd fade from memory and when it came time to get signatures on ballots, he'd be hopeless.

He needed publicity.

It didn't take long for me to figure out how to deliver it.

The key was Candidate 16.

The last time around, we'd selected Candidate 16 in a hurry. We'd been rushed. We'd gone with a simple solution. But this time around, we could do so much more. We were going to ask for submissions. We were going to ask people to nominate themselves for the 16th spot. And then we'd choose from among them.

The whole thing started with Information Technology. We were going to get huge numbers of submissions, we needed to narrow them down somehow. So, I started by building systems. We built online forms, we loaded up simulated profiles. And then we worked out how to narrow them down, automatically. We built tools to filter out those who weren't old enough, whose personal details didn't match public databases, who had been convicted of any crimes or even whose submissions had too many grammar or misspellings in their accompanying essays. We wanted colorful candidates, but not ones who couldn't be taken a *little* seriously. That first step took us the better part of a year. But by then, we were pretty confident we had the systems we needed.

When we were ready, on one of his appearances, Freddie announced that we would be launching a national search for the 16th candidate. We'd invite submissions from *anybody*. And we'd filter through them and choose the most interesting people we could – the people who would add the most to our national discourse. We'd then downselect to a narrow list of perhaps 150 people.

And then, and this is key, Freddie would travel to meet them and interview them. He'd do it on a weekly show: *The 16th Candidate*.

For us, that was the point. Freddie would be out there, every week. He'd be seeing the country and the country would be seeing him. He'd be listening to all sorts of colorful views. He'd be *seen* finding common ground across the spectrum. He'd be showing just how divided the country was and he'd even mention, occasionally, how badly it needed a true unifier. When he finally announced his own candidacy people would know that he understood *them*. He'd have the likability and the name recognition he'd need. Everybody would think that he was perfect.

Of course, when Freddie announced his own candidacy, he'd resign as host of the show and from any imaginary managerial role. To get his spot, he'd have to win it just like anybody else. He'd have to poll well in our all-star like system. Not that, by then, it should have been hard to do. He'd get his spot, and we'd have 15 candidates.

And the 16th Candidate? As before, the 16th Candidate would be announced on the first night of *Choose your Leader*.

Once the IT was ready, Freddie kicked things off. We got *millions* of submissions. We set a three-month deadline and they poured in the entire time. Freddie talked about the numbers, about the excitement. And then we filtered them. The actual filtering took hours, but Freddie drew it out over months. He made it look like we were being very careful, which we were. We managed to cut the millions down about 50,000. It is amazing how bad people's spelling can be and how many foreigners want to President of the United States. Finally, we hired a cadre of about 50 actual – human – reviewers. A whole lot of them were like the interns of the past, eager for a shot at mattering even if it meant taking on low-paying, short-term, work. In a week, they'd read every submission and flagged those who were remotely interesting. Reviews followed reviews and, in another week,, I had a short list of 150 potential candidates. 150 interesting, weird, and quixotic people with distinct political ideas. 150 people willing to be picked apart on the national stage for a shot at what Charlotte Morris had: fame.

The next stage was simple. Begin to visit the candidates. It would take a year. A year with a small film crew, a big bus and a whole lotta driving. It would be part political show and part loving travelogue of the country. Along the way we'd interview interesting and somewhat disturbed people.

And Freddie, of course, would be the host.

And so here we are, halfway across America (at least from a candidate perspective). Halfway across America and our busses have rolled to a stop.

I look out the window of the van. There's a house there. It's run-down, the windows are broken and it seems abandoned. There's a little yard with what appears to be a little tombstone in it. Otherwise, it's surrounded by empty space, just grass in every direction.

It is the last remnant of a neighborhood long since flattened by the municipal government of Detroit, Michigan.

According to our data, the Candidate is old enough at thirty-six. His spelling and grammar are perfect. And nobody understands his ideas.

I look at my phone again, just to make sure the address is accurate. It is.

I get out of the van and my film crew does the same.

We have no idea what we're about to encounter.

All we have is a name and an address.

A legal name and a verified address.

And, yes, we're really about to interview Mr. Everyone.

I have a feeling he might just make the perfect #16.

The Knock

Like all the other segments, the segment featuring Everyone will largely be worked out in advance. In other words, we'll sit with the candidate and figure out what we're going to talk about and stage it all a bit so it goes more smoothly. It just works better for TV.

Nonetheless, we wanted the introductions to be more real – to actually be spontaneous.

It is hard to fake the total surprise of getting the chance to run for President.

So, we get a single camera ready and then Freddie and I walk up to the door. I'm out-of-shot, but Freddie isn't. He's – no matter what we say about the candidates – the star of the show.

With a smile all ready, he knocks on the door. We expect it to open, at least a crack. But that's not what happens. Instead, we hear a whisper voice from within.

"Who is it?"

The accent is hard to place, like a pile of slight speech impediments stacked one on top of the other.

Freddie glances at the camera and then announces, in a confident tone, "Freddie Samuels, from *The 16th Candidate.*"

A moment later, the door opens. But just a crack. We see a fraction of a face peer through. We wait a moment. And then the voice says, in that same whisper, "Her."

"What?" says Freddie.

"I'll talk to her, no cameras."

We just glance at each other, a little taken aback. It is a little odd for a wannabe contestant to refuse to come on camera.

Freddie asks me, "You up for it?"

I turn to the crack in the door. "Alone?" I ask.

"Alone," says the voice, quietly.

Freddie jumps in, "We can just leave."

I think back over the man's submission. I've basically memorized it. It didn't seem dangerous. And it did check the other boxes: interesting and weird with distinct political ideas. It seems worth the risk.

"No," I say, "I'll do it."

With that, the door opens a bit more and the voice says, quietly, "Please, come in."

I turn to Freddie and with a bit of a lilt in my voice I say, "If I don't come back in 15 minutes, send in the cavalry."

He just grimaces. I don't think he thinks it's funny.

A moment later, I step through the door and the man inside closes it behind me.

My eyes take more than a moment to adjust. The house is dark. It is dark and dusty. The windows are covered by drapes and there are no lights on anywhere. If the place looked abandoned from the outside, then the inside has done very little to change that impression.

I turn and then I see Everyone. He's tall and thin. He might have been attractive, but instead he's dressed in clothes that fit him poorly. They seem dirty and old. He's not wearing glasses, but he seems to squint to see me. Although he isn't really looking at *me*. He's more focused on my feet. He's actually shaking, a bit. And he *smells*, strongly, of body odor.

I doubt he's had a bath in a month.

"S-Sorry," he says, looking down, "I don't have many visitors."

"No problem," I say, trying not to wince at the power of his smell.

He turns away and walks towards a closed door.

"Do you want me to come?" I ask.

He nods quickly, and so I do.

He reaches the door. There's a combination lock there. He presses a key and it lights up. Then he presses a few more and I hear a release of some sort of mechanism.

He pulls on the door and it opens, light streaming out from behind it. I look past him and I see a gleaming white staircase, leading downwards.

His eyes still shifting around, he says, "Let's talk in the basement?"

It is a question, not a statement.

I get the feeling the guy is a cliché collection of warning signs. There are so many of them I begin to hope that, in another 15 minutes, the TV crew outside will *actually* call the cavalry.

Nonetheless, I'm hooked.

Dutifully, I follow him down the gleaming staircase.

The Basement

The basement seems to have nothing in common with the house above it. It looks like a rich survivalist's bunker. There are stacks of canned food. Gleaming metal surfaces. Large computer monitors. A bed folded up against a wall and even a small treadmill. Somebody, I realize, could live down here for years.

I'm still looking around when Everyone clears his throat.

"I'm not sure where to begin," he says, in that weird, quiet, voice of his.

"Do you live down here?" I ask.

He kind of shakes his head a bit. Not a 'no', not a 'yes', more of a nervous tick. His eyes pull wide open, with a trace of fear.

"Do you need to know that?"

"No, no," I say, "I was just curious."

There's an uncomfortable pause. And then I ask, "So, why'd you sign up for *The 16th Candidate*?"

"They need me," he says, simply.

"Who?" I ask.

"Everyone," he says.

"Everyone needs you?" I ask.

He nods, quickly. Somehow, he pulls himself a little closer to the corner of the room.

I don't want to trigger anything violent, so I ask – as gently as I can, "*Why* does everyone need you?"

He takes a big breath, seeming to gather his strength, and then he blurts, "They have so much potential. But so much is being lost. They are suffering, even if sometimes they don't know it."

"And....," I ask, "Where exactly do *you* come in."

His eyes shift from side to side across the floor in front of me.

"I can help," he says.

"*How?*" I ask, my patience beginning to run thin.

"I'm Everyone," he says.

I just stare at him. This is getting nowhere.

"You changed your name to Everyone. Okay. So what?" I ask.

I want to add 'you freak.' I can find lots of weirdos with strange names, it doesn't mean I should put them on national TV.

"I didn't change my name," he says, "My mother named me that."

Now, that is odd.

"What? Why?"

I see him thinking, calculating. Then he finally answers. His eyes shifting to the side he says, "I-I don't know."

This man is not national TV material.

He continues, "She was worried people would want to hurt me. She came here to be safe."

"*Here?* Detroit? When?"

"When I was five. 30 years ago."

"Your mother had a strange idea of 'safe'."

"I've heard about the crime," he says, "But I've never seen it."

"Well, there isn't much now. The whole neighborhood is gone. But 30 years ago... well, they used to make movies about how dangerous this place was."

"That's probably why she picked it," he says, "She thought it would throw them off."

"Who's them?" I ask.

"I don't know," he says, "Whoever she was afraid of."

This guy isn't 16th Candidate material. He's scared, shifty, weird and has no qualifications whatsoever.

"I've got to go," I say.

His eyes pop up to mine, for just a second. There's desperation in them. And, fascination?

"WAIT!" he says.

"Why?" I ask.

"Because *they* need me. *Everyone* needs me."

"Give me a reason why they need you." I say, "Tell me what makes *you* the person they need."

He looks confused for a second.

"Isn't it obvious?" he says.

"No," I say.

"They need me because I *am* Everyone."

That again. I turn to leave, again. But he shoots his arm out and touches me, for just a fraction of a second.

"Wait, wait," he says, backing off apologetically, "I have a theory about the world."

"Go ahead," I say.

"People like to be divided into lots and lots of tribal groups. They break apart. And then they see everything from the eyes of their group. They can't understand each other so they're being torn apart" He looks at me, expectantly.

"Okay...?" I say. He looks confused, like he doesn't understand why I don't understand.

"Well... I, I don't have that problem. I can see things others can't."

This guy is sounding a bit like Freddie. I don't need a freaky, weirdo, Freddie. The one is enough. I shift, just a touch, back towards the door.

"What's your name?" he asks, suddenly.

"Amber," I say, pausing reluctantly.

He closes his eyes and bites his lower lip. And then he opens them and says, "Amber, I haven't stepped foot outside of this house in 30 years."

I just stare at him.

"In fact, this is the first face-to-face conversation I've had in all that time – except with my mother."

I'll give the man credit. He's managed to move from weird to *exceptionally* weird. That *could* be good for ratings.

"Why not?" I ask.

"I'm afraid," he says.

"Afraid?"

"My mother was afraid. That's why we came here. She told me not to leave. She told me it was dangerous. So, I've stayed."

"For 30 years?"

He nods.

Then he blurts, "I've learned a lot in those 30 years!"

"Like what?" I say.

"Like how to see things from everyone's perspective. How to fix things. How to help people do more of what they can with their lives."

"Really?" I say. My voice is dripping with doubt.

"Yes!" he says, "Ideas that aren't from the right or the left. Ideas that aren't from the middle. I've got ideas that are from, well, someplace else entirely. Simple ideas. But ideas that can help."

He certainly isn't Freddie.

And there is a possible storyline. A young man raised separate from humanity, as if by wolves. A city disappearing from around him. But he's been watching us the whole time. Studying us. And figuring out what we need to free us from any chains that bind us.

I wonder if his ideas involve space aliens. That could nix it.

"Give me an example."

"The national debt," he blurts.

"What about it?"

He sets off like a rocket, "Well, Alexander Hamilton said a national debt was useful because then other nations would be invested in your survival. But what if we issued national *equity* instead. Instead of getting fixed payments into the future – payments that can get too large for the nation to afford – investors would get a set slice of our GDP. If we grow, their payments grow. And if we face difficulties, those payments shrink. This way we'll never owe more than we can afford and we'll have a keen understanding of what that money really costs us – a percentage of everything we earn. Like a national tax. So, we'll be more careful. And the investors? The investors won't just be buying in to our survival. They'll be buying in to our success."

I just look at him. The idea is a little wonkish and definitely weird. But maybe it is just close enough to this side of crazy to spark some strong online discussion and debate and leave the viewers happy.

It might actually work.

"You have other ideas?"

"Yes, yes," he says, "About healthcare, education, taxes, mortgage financing, monetary policy, welfare, foreign policy – everything! They're all different. New. Ideas only somebody like me could have."

I purse my lips and then I ask, "Aren't you afraid."

"Yes," he says.

"So why do it?"

"I – I can't let them suffer."

The answer is heartfelt and simple. And in that moment, his eyes lift up and look straight at mine. I am shocked by how intense they are. I catch my breath in surprise.

"You understand, right?" he says.

In that moment, I think I do. Although, really, I know I don't.

A moment later his eyes shift back down to the floor.

"Everyone," I say, softly.

"Yes," he says.

I extend my hand, "I'll do my best to get you on the show."

"Thank you," he says.

He reaches, slowly, to shake my hand. I take his. It is greasy and unwashed. He shakes my hand, but only for a fraction of a second, and then he withdraws – pulling away from me.

I watch him, curious about this strange man. And then I turn, head up the stairs and walk through the dusty and dark house.

Finally, I step out to the sunny emptiness of a once-thriving Detroit neighborhood.

"So?" asks Freddie.

I look to make sure the cameras are off. And then I turn to Freddie and say, under my breath, "I think he might be #16."

Twenty-Five

I look at the circled date on the calendar again. January 2nd.

It is hanging on the gleaming metal wall of my basement; a reminder of my pain. For most people, January 2nd is just a date. But for me, it is the most important date.

It is the date my mother died.

I wasn't like other people. We weren't like other people. We didn't have a community; we only had each other. We lived in a house in Detroit and we never left. We were hiding. We had no friends. I had no friends. All she had was me. And all I had was her.

She did everything she could to teach me. But then she got sick and as she got weaker and weaker, I began to take care of her.

Until, one morning, January 2nd, she just wasn't there anymore.

I was only 11 years old. Thankfully, she'd never been a large woman and the sickness had only made her slighter.

Nonetheless, what came next wasn't easy. I took our wheelbarrow, which she'd used to take care of the vegetable garden, and I rolled her out of her bed and into it. I then wheeled her outside, just to the back of the house. I remember looking in every direction worried that some nosy neighbor would be poking their heads over our fence – or that some drone high above would be watching what I was doing. But nobody was watching.

At first, I thought I'd be quick about it. I thought I'd just dig a hole and bury her. But that wasn't what happened. The earth was hard. It was nearly frozen. And I was 11 years old.

I remember attacking the ground with that shovel. Not calmly, but furiously. Like I was angry at it. And I remember it not giving me an inch that I didn't take. It took three days to dig a hole deep enough for my mother's body. Three days. By the end my knuckles were bloodied, every limb in my body ached, and there was no more fury that I could muster. I was spent.

I buried her. I covered her body. And then, I went back inside.

Those three days were dangerous enough.

My mother had taught me well. I knew how to use the bank online, while covering my tracks. I knew how to order groceries with a credit card in the alias she borrowed. I knew how to read and how to write.

I knew how to survive.

And for those first years, that's all I did. I survived. I moved to the basement of our little house. I curled up into a ball and I cried. I ate what I needed to. And I survived.

My mother, the only person in my life, was gone.

All I could do was survive.

I used the Internet in those early days. But my mother had warned me of its dangers. There were predators there. There were people who would do me harm. I was not to go beyond the boundaries of what I needed to survive. But one day I clicked a link. It was some kind of news story. I figured it would be okay. It would be safe. And I read what came up. I can't remember now what it was. But I do know it was painful. Maybe a murder or a house fire. Something local that most people wouldn't have cared about. But I cared. I didn't have the thick skin some people developed from reading the news. Instead, I was drawn into the story and into the pain. I cried over that story; a story that involved people I'd never met. And then I did something else. I tried to think of ways to make the situation better. There was death involved, I remember that.

46

That could not be made better. So, soon enough, I tried to think of ways in which that story needn't have happened.

And for that moment, I forgot about my own pain.

I sought out the pain of others, I embraced it. I washed myself in it. All so that I could forget my own.

But that wasn't enough.

When I was little, my mother read me the Count of Monte Cristo. I remembered the story of Edmond Dantes and his 14 years in prison. I remembered all the things he learned. All the abilities he acquired. He had one man as a resource.

But I had a world at my fingertips.

That's why I decided I had to learn. I was going to click the links, read the stories, study the world. I'd be smart about it. Anonymous. I'd never post or comment or expose myself in any way. But I'd learn.

That's what I did. I watched the world through my screen. And then I bought another screen and another. I cleaned up the basement of that house. I secured it, just in case I attracted unwanted attention. I learned how to hack. How to write. How to analyze. And I watched. Not the world's joys, but the world's pains. The lost lives, which were easy to see. And the lost opportunities, which were far harder to see, but often more tragic.

And I dreamed of making it all better. But I was too afraid to leave. The world was okay as a distraction, not as a reality.

I didn't want the reality.

There was a song my mother liked. I changed the lyrics a bit, but they rang true for me.

I am living in a tin can

Far above the world

Planet Earth is blue

And there's nothing I can do

It was a song about an astronaut floating away from the world. That astronaut was me.

I wanted to help the world. I wanted to actually help the pain. But I knew I was powerless. After all, who was I? Some lost and confused man? Some hopeless person who would never belong?

I would never have the power to change anything. All I had were ideas that nobody would ever hear.

And so, I stayed in my cold lifeless world. Drifting further and further from the world. As the song said, 'Though I'm past one hundred thousand miles, I'm feeling very still.'

For 24 years, and counting, I had not stepped outside my door.

And then I saw the call for submissions to the 16th Candidate.

Aside from doing what I needed to survive, it was the first time I ever acted in the world. It was the first time I'd ever reached out. It was the first time I ever thought I could have helped it. Not that I expected anything to come of my submission.

On some level, it was just meant as another distraction. Another excuse not to do anything more reasonable; something that had a chance of coming to fruition.

But then I saw them on my cameras, the people from the show. And then they knocked on my door. I didn't want to answer it. But when I opened that door, just a crack, I saw her.

I know what people consider beautiful. I know she didn't fit the bill. But she had something else. She was vibrant. She was alive. *She was the first person I knew I could trust.*

I brought her into my house. Into my space capsule. I didn't really know how to talk to her. I didn't really know what she wanted. For all my practice speaking and listening to myself, I didn't really know how to communicate.

But I didn't want her to leave. I was watching her from the corner of my eye and I didn't want her to leave.

She was so full of life.

And I could be too.

When she selected me for the show, she sent a car.

And now it is waiting outside my house.

It is waiting for me to emerge.

It is January 2nd and I have been here 25 years.

I walk upstairs. I open the door.

And, shaking with fear, I step outside.

The Video

I'm sitting in the production booth watching the stages below. For this cycle's show, we've gone big. We've rented the Washington Wizard's Capital One arena. We've closed off most of it. Only one quarter of it is open, and it is stuffed with fans. Except, they aren't sports fans. They are political junkies and campaign supporters liberally salted with prominent politicians and high-profile businessmen. They have paid well for the privilege of being there.

The production booth itself is a tiny room, mounted near the luxury boxes (and, yes, we rented those out too). It is lit only by the images on the many computer monitors and video screens that fill the tight space. Monitoring everything is critical. Unlike most reality shows, this one will be running live.

We do a two-minute intro video and then each candidate will appear alone to answer the same softball question: "What is your signature issue?" They get three minutes to answer it and then we break for two minutes of ads.

The show will move incredibly quickly. There is a little time for filler, but in 15 minutes, we'll run 2 candidates and in 30, we'll run 4. Switching that quickly either requires some serious speed (which invites mistakes) or some serious cheating.

We've opted to cheat.

The stage the crowd sees is only one quarter of the platform it is mounted on. There are actually four stages, separated by high walls. The platform rotates, showing one quarter of the stage at any one time.

That quarter is the live stage. Instead of rushing, we can prep candidates for over 20 minutes, rotate them in front of our live audience (the TV audience doesn't see this), interview them, and then replace them with the next warm body and smoothly polished voice by rotating the stage once more.

Bam. Bam. Bam.

The operation is so smooth it gives me goose bumps.

The crowd is here and, down below, the staff are getting ready for the first candidates of the first night. The place is a flurry of activity. It would seem simple – just plop a night-show style desk and couch on each of the stages, set up some lighting, manage some timing and you're set. But this isn't some bare bones talk-show. Sure, we've got swooping cameras, crowd shots and all the rest. But what's really critical is that we've got *candidates*. There are 16 candidates waiting for their chance to pitch to the country as a whole. Most of them have raised millions or tens of millions of dollars. So, of course, they have handlers. Instead of having 16 guests to prep (itself a seriously difficult proposition), we have 16 guests and something close to 300 of *their* staff running around making sure everything is just right. We've got to manage *their* people, not just our own.

Trust me when I say that the place is crazy.

But it is all running just as it is supposed to.

Everything has happened, just as planned. Two months earlier, Freddie announced that he would be seeking the highest office in the land. His speech was right on point: "We need a unifier. We need somebody who respects *all* America has to offer. We need to focus less on ideology and more on people." Yada yada yada, it was perfect. He not only announced his candidacy, he told everybody his interests in *Choose your Leader* would be placed in a trust and another host would be hired for the upcoming competition. He was open and frank and people ate it up. Helping him along, the sitting President decided not to seek reelection, due to health issues.

Oh, and the competition to replace him as host was serious – it was suddenly seen as a path to the Presidency.

We didn't even need to pay the next guy.

The week *before* Freddie's announcement a poll had compared him, as a hypothetical candidate, with all the known candidates. He stacked up pretty well. But after that little speech, only 2-minutes in length, he dominated.

What followed was a flurry of signature campaigns to get him on various state ballots. He wasn't a Democratic or Republican. But he needed to be one of the two to show up on major state ballots. The Democratic party had a higher rate of voter identification, and so Freddie became a Democrat. He became a Democrat and he shot to the top of their polls. My future was looking good.

And I know, I know, that I'm not supposed to favor anybody. After all, the show prided itself on supporting the campaigns themselves – all the campaigns. It was how we got the candidates to sign on. But nothing was going to stop me from putting in that extra effort when it came to Freddie. *Choose your Leader* wasn't going to make itself an obstacle to a President Freddie Samuels.

Plus, Freddie had been growing on me. He might not have had managerial chops or any particular ideology – but he could certainly bring people together. The *16th Candidate* had demonstrated that. People, all kinds of people, saw how Freddie interacted with people *like them*. And they loved it. He was respectful of everybody. It helped, of course, that we chose people he could be respectful of. Nonetheless, he laughed at nobody – not even gently. It seemed like, in his mind, *any* American could have been a decent 16th Candidate.

Because of that, darned near every American thought Freddie respected them. He was exactly what he aspired to be: the kind of agreeable clown the country needed. We could do a lot worse.

As I sit in the booth, I watch the cameras carefully – *all* the cameras. We have them everywhere. We've made the locker rooms and offices into dressing rooms (people aren't actually getting dressed there) and I've got eyes on them all. It's all so that I can get help wherever it's needed, immediately.

As I scan the stages and the 'backstage', I see the candidates with their bundles of handlers and assistants. And then I see Freddie in his dressing room. He's there, by himself. And he's just sitting, placidly, watching his reflection in the mirror. I know he likes what he sees. And I know he thinks there's nothing he needs to work on.

The fact is, he might just be right.

But he isn't the only Candidate without handlers.

Sitting alone, in his own dressing room, is Candidate 16. He isn't confident. His head is in his hands and he's gripping his hair tightly. He's a wreck; nervous and scared.

I chose him, but even now I'm not sure that was the right thing to do. The problems began as soon as I invited him to come to D.C. The dude had never been out of his house. Not since he was five at least. He'd never been in a car or a bus or an airplane. He'd never crossed a street. He had no idea how to get around.

He didn't even have ID.

There were definitely some practical issues to overcome.

So, I sent a car and driver and they picked him up and they drove him back to D.C. The driver told me Freddie sat silently, just staring out the window like a kid in a candy store. I could picture it –

suddenly seeing all that space and all those people after a lifetime in a single room.

The driver dropped him off at our offices in Georgetown. I met him at the curb. Thankfully, he'd taken a shower and given himself a hair-cut. But he didn't fit otherwise. He wore clothes only a blind man could love (and even then, self-respect would have led that blind man to ask *somebody* to give him some decent advice). And he seemed to want to disappear, somehow curling up into himself as he stood on the street side. When I invited him into the building, he shot forward; like he was eager to escape the open space.

I had thought about putting him up in a hotel, but I realized it just wouldn't work. He'd just sit there, in the room, and never leave. I needed somebody who could do a passable job as a candidate.

I had to get him ready for his 5 minutes of fame.

I brought him back up to the office. I looked around the largely open space. I knew everybody's job. I knew what they were working on. As I scanned the room, I realized that none of them had any time for Everyone.

And then I saw an unfamiliar face. She was a young and chipper looking blond woman. Probably an intern. She was having a coffee in the breakroom. I walked Everyone over towards her.

"You," I said, directing my voice at her.

Her eyes popped up.

"Uh, yeah?" She asked.

"I need you to take care of this guy," I said, gesturing at Everyone.

She looked at me, then at him.

"But-" she said. Then she thought better of it. "Okay, how?"

I looked her up and down. She was dressed well, her speech was good, her eyes bright and curious.

"He needs clothes, he needs a speech therapist, he needs glasses, some dental work, a decent haircut – the Flowbee doesn't cut it. And he needs to talk to people, okay?"

"Uh, okay," said the woman.

I thought a moment longer.

"You'll have to move into my house, with him. He's gonna need a lot of work." I pulled a spare key off my keychain and handed it to her.

"Okay," said the woman.

"You know where I live?"

She shook her head, no.

I gave her the address.

Just then, a head, belonging to one of the graphic designers (another fashionable young woman), popped up over a cubicle wall. "Rachel, we can go now."

"Just a moment," said the woman (evidently Rachel) as she held up a finger. "I think I just got a job."

Evidently, she wasn't one of the interns.

I had my secretary get a couple of pairs of glasses with discrete cameras hidden in them. I wanted to get some footage of Everyone; I do run a TV show after all. For her part, Rachel did her job superbly well. By the time I got home from work, Everyone was wearing decent clothes, had a nice haircut, a new set of glasses and a series of appointments scheduled with a woman who was apparently the best speech therapist in the city.

But he still seemed scared of *everything*.

When she got me alone, Rachel asked, "Is he a homeless guy you're, uh, rescuing?"

I smiled at her.

"No," I said, "Don't tell anyone, but he's the 16th Candidate."

That night, I took him out for dinner. He didn't want to go. He didn't see why it was necessary. But I told him that if he was too frightened of people, they would never vote for him. He had to learn if he wanted to help.

And so, he came along - reluctantly. He stuck to me, close to me, like I was protecting him somehow. I tried to encourage him to at least *pretend* not to be so frightened. It had a little bit of an effect, but not much of one. I still couldn't get him to make eye contact, with me or anybody else.

We only had a few weeks to go. As we ate, I grew increasingly concerned this wasn't a good idea. I was thinking that maybe I could still find a housewife with some radical views.

After dinner, we left the restaurant. And on the way back, there was a woman walking down the street. Her eyes were red from crying. It was then that Everyone did the most remarkable thing. As I watched with my camera glasses, he pulled himself away from me and walked up to her. She looked up as he approached. He said something, but he was too far away to hear.

I saw her smile. And then she spoke to him, briefly. She smiled through fresh tears. He said something else. And she gave him a hug. He accepted it awkwardly. Then she moved on, walking away with an expression of – I don't know – emotional refreshment.

"What was that?" I asked.

He didn't answer. And then I saw that he had tears of his own.

We got back to the house, a cozy Colonial in Chevy Chase.

Rachel was there. She asked me if I needed anything. I didn't. She asked Everyone if he needed anything. He didn't.

And just like that, a routine was established.

During the day, Rachel worked with him. Bit by bit, his speech improved. Bit by bit, he seemed a little less frightened. And bit by bit I began to think that maybe it wouldn't all go horribly wrong.

Of course, I didn't want it to horribly right, either. Everyone was there to fail. We didn't want the established candidates – or Freddie – to actually be threatened by him. He just had to look credible enough that it seemed like the 16th Candidate was meant to be something other than comic relief.

As the weeks passed, Everyone kept close to me. He seemed to trust me more than he trusted Rachel. Not that I deserved it. After all, he was meant as a stage prop. He was not meant to be what *he* thought he was; a real candidate.

Nothing brought this more to life than his 2-minute introductory video. On the video, we had to talk him up. After all, *we chose him.* But we also had to build in his fatal flaw. We had to have the narrative bit that would explain why primary voters shouldn't go for him. It would help with the drama and it would prime the social media conversations. More importantly, the other candidates wouldn't be pleased if our 'color' choice knocked them out of the race.

It wasn't hard to pick one. He was weird. Very very weird. We crafted his story so that he would be so strange that nobody would identify with him – and nobody would think he could really identify with them. His whole Everyone persona would be subtly turned inside out.

The video we made was great. It started with the camera running over the emptiness of his Detroit neighborhood and then entering his mother's house and making its way down to the gleaming basement. The voiceover described a great discovery in an unlikely place. A singular, brilliant, man who spent his life studying others, but from a distance. It would describe a man seeing solutions for the problems facing America. A man trying to become what his mother named him: Everyone.

Everyone approved of the video. But he didn't understand it. He didn't realize that after watching the video, American wouldn't see Everyone. Instead, they'd see No One.

One round and he would be done; sacrificed in the name of a higher purpose.

About a week before the show, I moved Everyone out. I got him a hotel room and I gave Rachel another job. By then, he knew what he needed to get around, by himself. He even had an ID.

I told myself that I was letting him be free. I was *pushing* him to be independent. But I knew the truth was a little different. I knew I was stranding him. I was stranding him so that when he got up on that stage, he'd be exactly what I needed him to be.

My plan was perfect.

But the scene with the crying woman kept playing back to me. He cared. He cared so much that he overcame his fear. Not just of her, but of the world. He cared so much that he let me lift him up – despite his fears. What he didn't know was that I was lifting him up just so I could throw him down.

After he left, I made another video. It was just an experiment. But it told another story. This video started in the basement. It spoke of his modest means. It talked about him never having entered the political game. The camera shifted to a video of him explaining something on a computer screen. There was no volume, but he was animated and involved. The voiceover explained he studied endlessly; because he was taught that you ought to know what you're talking about before you opened your mouth. Then the video mourned that his chance to talk never came, at least not until the *16th Candidate* came knocking at his door.

Next, the video cut to the scene of an interview. Only one person was on camera, and it wasn't him. Instead, it was the crying woman he'd spoken to on the street. I'd had Rachel track her down. And on a large monitor in the room, there was the video of Everyone comforting her. I trimmed it down to 10 seconds. When it stopped, the off-camera interviewer (me actually) asked the crying woman what she'd thought about the man she'd hugged. As the camera zoomed in on her she smiled, the tears streaming once again. And she said, "I don't who he was. He came out of nowhere. But he cared. And, he gave me hope."

Finally, the video drew away from his basement, through his house and out to a view of his home standing alone in an erased Detroit neighborhood.

The tagline was simple: "Candidate Everyone, standing strong for you."

I made the video, but I didn't do anything with it. Instead, even now, I'm keeping it on a little thumb drive in my pocket. It is just a what if. It isn't something I could ever *really* use.

Candidate by candidate, the evening unfolds. Candidate after candidate has their videos run. Candidate after candidates takes their three minutes to tell America what *their* signature policy is. I'd prepped Candidate Everyone for this. I told him to go into the weeds and to focus on the technical. I set him up for failure. He wasn't going to look *quite* human.

But he doesn't know any better, so it'll okay – right?

His naivete made it all so easy. And, it makes it all so hard.

As candidate after candidate comes on screen, I feel a sense of dread growing in me. All of them know what they are doing. They all know why they are there.

None of them is being set up for anything.

None of them, but 16.

Candidate 10. 11.

Soon it will be Candidate Everyone's turn. Then, there'll be nothing I can do to undo what I'd already done.

12 comes and goes. Candidate Everyone steps up to his part of the rotating stage.

13 and 14. The stage rotates, again and again. Time is running out. But I have a show to support, right? 16 isn't a real candidate. He's just a part of the show, right? He has a role to play, that's all I've given him. A role. A part. He has to know that.

And he'll play it perfectly.

The stage rotates again and it is Freddie's turn. The crowd erupts in applause. Candidate 15, Freddie, is everybody's favorite.

I watch him. So smooth, so aware. He knows exactly what his words will accomplish. His smile. His every motion sells *him*. He doesn't need any help. Everybody loves him.

But 16? 16 needs help. 16 *needs* somebody in his dressing room. As soon as we break for the ads, I watch the stage begin to rotate. I see Everyone's face as he is moved in front of the massive crowd. His eyes open in all-consuming fear and he grips his chair; locked up and unable to move. I'm suddenly compelled to do *something*.

In a mad dash, I run down to the stage and then up and on to it while it is still rotating him into position. The bright lights are suddenly warm on my back. I can feel the crowd wondering what I'm doing. I dash to Everyone's chair. His eyes snap to mine as he realizes that I'm there. I look him in the eye, those intense eyes, and I say: "Forget what I said about details, about policy. Make it human. Keep it simple. And just pretend there's absolutely nobody here."

He looks right at me. Confused at first. Maybe he knows I'd been manipulating him. But then he closes his eyes and I know that he is thinking.

I run back towards the booth. The show is coming back on – the 3-second video 'splash' announcing the end of the ad break comes on. I can hear the audio throughout the arena.

I pull the thumb drive from my pocket as I run.

The host (not Freddie) starts speaking. He announces that we were back with the person everyone has been waiting for: "Candidate 16." His introduction is 25 seconds long. I know it by heart. I run as fast I can and as I burst into the booth, I hand the thumb drive to a Tech. "Run this instead!" I almost shout.

The tech looks at me. He blurts, "But the candidate –"

I know what he's going to say, "The candidate hasn't approved it."

I hear the host announce "And now, his introductory video!"

"Run this, **instead**!" I demand. There is an edge of steel in my voice. The tech grabs the drive from my hand.

The host looks confused. No video is up. The TV broadcast goes dark. 1, 2, 3 seconds go by.

Tens of millions of people are watching. There's a blank screen and it feels like eternity.

And then, finally, my *new* video comes on.

And after exactly 2 minutes, it comes to an end.

I've done my part.

The camera return to the host. Candidate Everyone is sitting there, still nearly frozen in fear, waiting for the question every candidate has faced.

"So," says the host in his buttery voice, "Tell me, what is *your* signature issue?"

The Signature

As I look at the cameras, I can see that none of the other candidates are paying any attention to #16. They're all in their own dressing rooms, talking with the staffs. They are doing serious campaigning, and they know #16 is just a side show. Even Freddie, who has no staff, isn't paying any attention. He trusts me. He trusts me so much that he's watching the video of his own performance. He's critiquing himself.

But me? I'm watching Everyone.

His eyes are darting across the room. Nervous. Uncertain. Unstable.

"Healthcare," he says, quietly.

"Sorry, I didn't hear that," says the host.

"Healthcare," Everyone says, more loudly. "Um..."

He bites his bottom lip.

"Um... when I was 11 years old, my mother was diagnosed with cancer. I – I remember when she came home. She told me the treatments for her condition could have extended her life for a few months. But she told me it would have cost us everything we owned. So..." he trails off, but then picks up again – his voice shaking, "So she decided *not* to be treated so that *I* could keep the house we lived in. When she died a few months later. I buried her in our backyard."

The crowd is silent. I just look at the screen in shock. None of the records showed that his mother died. But it all makes sense. The upstairs of the house hasn't been touched in years. It is coated with dust. This man, Everyone, has been *alone* for 25 years. Totally alone. I can hardly imagine what that was like.

With his introduction, a few of the other candidates have begun to turn towards their monitors. They've begun to watch. I don't know if is because they are curious or if it is because their animal instincts sense a threat.

And then Everyone continues, his voice a bit stronger:

"Today, that same cancer can be treated with a 95% success rate *because* companies invested billions in the hope of making money on more effective treatments. As the treatments got better and better, I kept wondering what if? I mean, if we'd had free healthcare 24 years ago, she would have had a few horrible months added to her life. But if she'd been diagnosed 24 years later, well – we'd have been even less able to afford the treatment. I – I didn't see a way, for anybody who was poor, to avoid the pain of what I went through. Either you make healthcare free and kill innovation, or you allow people to charge whatever a life is worth and price those whose lives are worth... less... right out of existence. We've taken the second path. We've paid for the world's healthcare innovation, but we ourselves often can't afford it. And I worry, that even today, my mother still wouldn't have survived."

He draws in a deep breath and then, he stands up – his hand gripped by his side.

"I knew there had to be a better way."

His voice is growing stronger, "There had to be a way to avoid the pain in the future. To save lives – even those we don't yet know how to save. And, and, I found one."

He smiles for a moment. And I see his eyes tearing up.

At that second, you could have heard a pin drop in that arena. Everybody is waiting for what Everyone will say next. The chatter in the dressing rooms has almost stopped. I glance at the social media dashboard; millions are watching, but nobody is saying anything at all.

And then Everyone continues: "It's simple really. If the government pays the median cost of any treatment, then we have a solution. If patients choose to spend more, maybe for private rooms, they can. But if they do, they'll pay the difference. But what's really important is that if they spend *less*, then *they* get to *keep* the difference. By shopping around, they can actually make themselves money. The patients, with their millions of individual decisions, will drive down the median costs of healthcare. And then those costs, and the resulting payouts, will be adjusted to reflect improved efficiencies.

"Think about it," Everyone says, with a broad smile, "With this, everyone will be able to afford healthcare *and* the free market will be harnessed to both drive down costs and improve quality.

"If health care is free, then no child's mother will be denied a cure we already have. And if we allow profits for healthcare innovation, then, eventually, no cancer will be uncurable. We can do both. And perhaps, some time in the future, no child will be left without their parent."

He looks around, expectantly. He's smiling. Joyful. Proud.

But nobody says anything. As the cameras zoom out to the crowd, there is no clapping or cheering. There are just people watching, taking in his words – processing what they've seen.

Ideas for everyone, I think wistfully.

I had no idea he really meant it.

Sanussi

As with most things political, my office isn't quite an open-plan affair. Instead, it is a comfortable 5th floor space with a view of Pennsylvania Avenue in Georgetown. As I look out my window, the sun bounces off the buildings opposite me and the traffic rushes by on the street below. It is a comfortable place to work. The building itself is old. It has smell of something comfortable with its age. Carpets, and wood and bricks that have seen their share of life – and are unlikely to be surprised by anything. I have wooden chairs and a solid wooden desk. My fancy-looking Barista certificate hangs on the wall. Few people notice it.

The building feels like it used to be a newspaper. Like the editors' offices in an old-time TV show, there are windows between my office and the rest of the floor. I suppose they're there so I can keep an eye on my 'journalists'. But, embedded in the windows, there are also blinds. I know they're there so that when I choose, I can keep the journalists from keeping an eye on me.

I've never closed those blinds. But now, as I look at my phone, I almost involuntarily stand up and make my way to them. There's a text message on my phone. It has a link; the kind of thing everybody knows you shouldn't click. It might be spam, but it might not.

I get to the blinds and pause, for just a moment. This can't be real can it? Then another message arrives, with another link, and I know that it is. I glance out my windows and then I close the blinds one at a time. I still don't know if I'll click the link. I won't get a virus, at least I know that. But a virus isn't the only thing to fear.

With the blinds closed, I slowly walk back to my desk. My eyes are on the screen the entire time. I absent-mindedly reach up and close the blinds overlooking the street. My office is cast into relative darkness.

I sit down in my chair, reluctantly.

And then, half a minute later, my finger hovers over the little patch of blue underlined text.

It may be stupid, but it's the only smart thing to do.

I know, looking at the message, that it's been sent because of the polls. Not the votes, the polls. The first time I'd run the reality show, I didn't care much about who voted for whom. I had no horse in the race and our 15th and 16th candidates were just willing sacrifices on the altar of ratings.

But this time it was different. This time, my future rode on Freddie. So, as the polls came in, I was glued to the TV in my office (when you're in entertainment, you can have a TV in your office). The official primaries distribute each party's delegates to the winning candidates in each state. But we don't. Instead, we count the total number of votes received, and *that* determines who makes it through to the Top Twelve. Of course, those who get delegates will make it through this round; you can't win a state and fall out of the top 12. But a lot of other candidates can also clear this particular hurdle.

As the results came in, I cared about how Freddie did. He was my future. But I also kept an eye on Everyone. I told myself that another round of Everyone could be ratings gold. And by the end of the day, it was clear *both* of them had made it through. Freddie captured an incredible 30% of the vote. And Everyone squeezed into the 12th spot with 2.3%. But both were through. Both were through, and I was delighted.

At least I was until the polls started coming in. I'd hoped Everyone would be labeled as a weirdo. I'd hoped that would limit his potential, and the threat that he posed.

But that wasn't what the polls showed. When one little polling outfit asked for words to describe him the answers ranged from "caring" to "smart" on the positive side of the ledger to "inexperienced" on the negative.

"Weird" wasn't even on the leader board.

And that's when I knew he was threat. We couldn't undo weird. But a little more exposure could fix inexperience.

Of course, I wasn't the only one who saw this. A whole lot of people discovered Everyone that night. In the weeks that followed that first batch of primaries, somebody started an official campaign and donations started pouring in. Soon afterwards, Everyone got on the ballot. In a few states, those no-name state parties that nobody ever votes for nominated him for their tickets. In most of the others, huge signature campaigns were launched. In those states, Everyone would show up under that most appropriate of groupings: "Independent."

It was when I was in my office, watching some political talking head pontificate on Everyone's chances that I received the text message.

It read only: "Chat over coffee click here".

I thought the message might be from Freddie, but I wasn't sure I could trust it. Lots of people chat over coffee, right?

But then came the second message: "Chat with Muammar here".

That's when I knew it was Freddie. He'd called himself Muammar in the ballroom, when he told me he was going to run. We weren't supposed to coordinate. If we were caught, the optics would be horrible; both Freddie and the show would suffer.

It would be stupid to click the link.

At the same time, though, I'd be an idiot *not* to reply to my future President.

With one more glance at my closed office blinds, I click the link. A private chat room (at least I think it's private) pops up.

Muammar? I ask.

The little ellipses blink on the page "...". Then, Freddie replies,

Sanussi?

I'm not quite sure who Sanussi is. But I can guess. He was probably Gaddafi's Chief of Staff.

Why are you reaching out?

He wasn't supposed to be a threat. 'He was supposed to be weird.

I know Freddie is talking about Everyone. But he's not just making a statement. He's asking a question: "What the hell happened?" All I did was tell him to make it personal. It wasn't much, right. But I can't admit I helped him because I didn't want to see him destroyed.

I thought it would be good for ratings

I'm not quite lying, I'm just being selective with my answer.

The campaign is more important than a little buzz for the show. Do you actually want to be Sanussi?

I can't imagine Gaddafi's Chief of Staff was a nice guy. But we're talking in code names, right? The fact is, Freddie is threatening the job he promised me.

I guarantee the weirdo is no threat

Freddie replies immediately:

You know better than that. You need to finish the job.

Even though Freddie can't see me, I nod my head. I need to finish the job. Everyone can't actually be a threat. It is time to take him off the board.

I will

When?

I know that, if I just abandon him for a little while, then Everyone will be done. He doesn't even need to know it is happening.

The next round

There's a long pause. Then Freddie replies:

Good

A moment later, the window closes and the chat disappears.

I stare at my screen, glowing brightly in the darkened room.

And then I think of Everyone and I wonder whether I have what it takes to do what I must.

The Top 12

The candidates and their campaign managers are all gathered in our conference room. It sits in the core of our office, far from any windows. The conference room is a closed off space. We can meet here, privately – surrounded by old (medium quality) wood-paneled walls, discount rugs, and a massive wooden conference table. There's a projector on and the lights are dimmed so that its image can be seen more easily.

There are 12 Candidates left. 12 candidates and 11 Campaign Managers. Freddie still doesn't have one, but Everyone has hired Rachel. I like her, but she's not exactly a high-powered choice.

But, then again, neither was I.

As I look around the darkened room, I see the faces of the Candidates and their managers lit up in the bright lights of their individual laptops. Only Freddie and Everyone have no computers. Only their faces are shrouded in darkness.

I hit a button on my computer and after a few seconds, my first slide comes up.

"The Top 12."

Faces turn towards me and I click the button again: "Separation Round."

"Welcome, Candidates," I begin. "The next round is the Domestic Crisis. This is the first time we are holding this particular challenge. This is a separation round. This means that those who are going through the challenge will be isolated from the other Candidates. This is to ensure that those who go later will *not* have more time to prepare for the crisis. If there are violations of this policy, if the candidates or their chosen advisors attempt to learn about the crisis in advance, then those Candidates will be removed from the show, no matter their primary vote performance. Any questions so far?"

Most of the candidates are sitting forward in their chairs, taking notes and watching carefully. Everyone isn't like them. He seems to pull away from the table, receding into the darkness. He's watching carefully, but most of what I see is confusion.

There are no questions, of course. The candidates are too cagey to share their questions and concerns in front of one another. Instead, I'm sure they're already emailing or texting me – hoping to somehow finagle an advantage over their competition. I sometimes feel like an overworked professor with a bunch of students unwilling to face the consequences of their sub-par work. Only instead of the students writing notes and begging me to adjust their grades, they have entire staffs trying to pull off the same trick.

I click the next slide: "The Process." A little diagram shows up alongside it.

"Okay. All the candidates and their selected domestic advisors will be in a shared soundproof chamber underneath the stands to start the process. It will actually be half the practice court, with sound dampening walls built within it. There will be microphones and one-way glass. The audience, both physically here and on TV, will be able to see and hear you at any time. But you will be unable to see or hear them. One-by-one candidates and their advisors will be taken from the shared soundproof space through the tunnel to the main arena where there will be another soundproof room set up on the stage. This room will be a replica of the Oval Office. It will be one-way glass on all sides. We'll be able to film you from any angle, but you won't be able to see outside. Shortly after you and your advisor arrive, a 'staffer' – really a paid actor from the show – will dash in and give you information about some kind of domestic crisis. Any questions?"

"Um... what kind of crisis?" It is Everyone's uncertain voice, calling out from the darkness and barely audible over the sound of the projector.

The expressions on the other candidates' faces (lit up by their laptops) seem annoyed by his interruption. He glances around the table, too aware of their reactions.

"I can't tell you," I say, "Because I don't know. The scenario is controlled by independent auditors."

"Okay," says Everyone, carefully.

"Okay," I say, "Moving on... the actor has particular lines to deliver and if you ask questions, he can answer them... if he's been given answers. Otherwise, he'll just say 'I don't know'."

"So, what do I do?" asks Everyone, again in a quiet and shaky voice.

Somebody in the room sniggers.

"Whatever you think is appropriate," I say. I add, thinking of Freddie, "But remember that the country will watch you do it."

"What do you mean appropriate?" asks Everyone. Smug faces turn in his direction. The other candidates have assembled teams just to answer that question.

"I can't tell you that either," I say, coldly. In reality, I suppose I could have told him anything I wanted to. But I won't. His competition will work out what they need to work out and he won't survive the second round.

"I will say," I continue, "That you have five minutes to do whatever you're going to do. After that time, you'll be moved out, to another secure room – the other half of the Arena's practice court.

75

This room won't be soundproof, but it will still be wired for video and audio. In addition, it will have a TV screen showing later candidates' responses to the Crisis. The audience will be able to see how you react to them."

Unspoken, but understood, is that the earlier candidates will get more screen time. It is a perk of doing well in the first round of primary voting. I imagine Everyone shirking in one of that room's corners. But he'll be the last candidate and won't spend any time there.

"When everybody has finished, the round will be over and we can all go watch the polling. Any final questions?"

This time, nobody speaks. But the fear has returned to Everyone's eyes.

I know what will happen next. The Candidates will all go back and war game the round – trying to figure out exactly how to react before they get on screen. They'll have varying degrees of success, but they'll all basically figure out what they need to be doing. They are professionals after all.

But Everyone? Everyone will fail spectacularly, and on national TV. And I'll have done exactly what Freddie told me to.

The campaign is more important than a tiny rating bump. And the campaign is more important than Everyone.

With one final glance around the room, I turn on the lights and thank the candidates for coming. One by one, they silently pack up their computers and leave the room. Whatever discussions they have will be held far from the other Candidates. Before long, only Freddie, Everyone and Rachel are there.

Freddie is silent. He's there to listen. And there's plenty to listen to; Everyone and Rachel are sitting there. Their voices are panicked as they try to figure out what this challenge is about and how to get through it.

I see Freddie smile. Then he tips his head to me and he leaves the room. If Rachel knew anything about politics, she might be able to figure this out. But she doesn't. Neither of them knows what's coming.

"This is Presidential politics," I tell myself, "It isn't a game for innocents or amateurs."

With that thought, I unplug my laptop, preparing to leave the room. Everyone glances at me. Then he notices my face, my expression, and his transforms. In that moment I see the care he had for the woman on the street. And I know that he's trying to reassure me. He's trying, in his way, to help me get through whatever I'm going through.

That only makes it worse.

The rest of my workday is not an easy one. I keep picturing Everyone being destroyed on national TV. I see him stuttering, uncertain, scared. Trapped. I see him as a mockery locked into a soundproof stage for five minutes like some circus freak.

It isn't a pleasant thought. I end up leaving the office early. I head down to the garage and pull open the door on my 15-year-old gray Honda Civic. I slide inside. The car smells like I've lived in it. I have, after all. Food, deodorant, body odor and the scent of unwashed clothes mingle together. The fabric on the seats is stained. A little "Minnesota Vikings" sticker is still stuck to the dashboard. It seems like I put that on there a millennia ago and in some different universe. The car, remarkably, feels like home. It reminds me of a simpler place.

I start the engine, it turns over as easily as ever. And then I pull the boring little car out of its spot and head into the nightmare that is D.C. traffic. I'm really heading anywhere. I'm just driving. And so I drive up Pennsylvania avenue, towards the White House. The numbers on the street click by, drawing ever closer to 1600. The traffic is moving at a crawl. It's okay. I'm not trying to get anywhere.

Up ahead I see the first of the security barriers. I can't drive up to the White House, I'll be routed around like every other subject. That white columned building is like some Emperor's Hidden Palace; separated from the world around it by some mystique and a great deal of actual security.

But it won't be that way for long, will it? In a few months, I'll be able to drive right up to the gate. And they'll let me in. I'll work there, as Freddie's Chief of Staff.

I smile at the idea, even as I wend my way around the barriers. This is the center of the Empire. And I'll be a part of its very core.

And then I wonder, for just a second, what Everyone sees on the streets of D.C. Does he see suffering? Does he see the schemes? Or is he just blind it all. And paranoid, like an old man, because he can't figure who or how people are trying to destroy him.

He fears them, I realize. He wants to help them. But he fears them. The only one he doesn't seem to fear is *me*. And I'm the one who's going to destroy him.

As I drive, I notice a woman carrying coffee and I imagine the shortcuts she's taken, and the people she's taken advantage of. It's the way you find your place in this city. Even if you show up pure of heart, the corruption will become a part of you. You won't even notice the choices make even as they both weigh you down and lift you up.

Does Everyone see the weakness in my soul?

Or does he see something better?

I keep driving. Hours later, I somehow myself pulling into an underground parking lot. I look up and see the sign over the entrance. I'm at the Georgetown Hotel. Everyone's hotel.

Almost automatically, I get my ticket, take a parking spot and then head to the lobby. The place is gorgeous, with a two-story atrium, inlaid wood floors, Persian carpets and Art Deco furniture scattered around in what is certainly a well thought-out pattern. Somehow the place is both open and airy, and cozy and close. I take another elevator up to Everyone's floor. The hallway is just as nice, with subdued and dark carpets, thick wooden doors and tastefully inlaid lighting.

I walk down it, locate Everyone's door and knock softly.

Rachel opens it. Is she staying here?

She certainly seems relieved to see me.

She invites me in. The place is huge, with a full living room and two attached bedrooms. I suppose it's all on the show's budget, or the campaigns. I'm not sure which.

The room's décor matches that of the lobby. There are fine inlaid wooden floors, Persian carpets, Art Deco furniture, and floor-to-ceiling windows (framed with lush dark-red curtains) that have a view of the Capitol.

I step inside. Everyone glances up and a broad smile crosses his face.

"I'm out of my depth," he says, "I don't know what I'm doing. I'm scared of the crowds. Of the open spaces. I think maybe I should just drop out and go home."

"Drop out?" I think, "That would work."

But, no, he can't just drop out. *I* want to hear what he has to say.

I want to hear what he has to say.

Rachel offers me water. I turn it away. I don't want anything from them. Not even a glass of water. If I took it, I think it'd make me feel sick. All I'm here to do is make sure he isn't totally embarrassed. I'm not here to help, not really.

"Here's the drill," I say, as coldly as I can manage, "When you get in there, talk to your advisor. Think about what to do. You have five minutes. Use them. A minute of thought will stop you from rushing into something stupid. Then, give orders, make a speech, whatever. You just need to react. You need to deal with the crisis. Okay?"

"Okay," Everyone and Rachel say.

"The most critical thing," I continue, "Is that you need to do it without alienating too many people."

Everyone looks hurt, "Why would I alienate *anyone*? I'm here to help them."

"Because that's how the scenarios *are designed*," I say, "They're meant to play on divisions in society. Race and identity, abortion, gun ownership. One of these types of things will come up. You've got to play it smart. If you hem and haw, you'll seem weak. You need to take a position. And in order to do so, you need to choose *which someone's* are the most important when it comes time to win an election."

Everyone just looks at me, confused.

"Gun owners or safety advocates, whites or blacks, religious Christians or humanists. Take your time to run the numbers in advance. Figure out who can carry you forward. And then say what *they* need to hear."

"Why do I need to do this?" Everyone asks.

"This is an Empire," I say, "The Emperor is in the business of handing out goodies. That's how you govern. You need to figure out what combination of goodies will get you what you want."

His face falls. He asks, "Is that what you do?"

The question hits me, hard. I don't answer it.

"Everyone," I insist, "This is what you need to do in order to win."

Suddenly, I'm not so sure it is worth winning. I could help him more, I realize. I could tell him to pretend the glass box is his little room. I want to tell him to speak slowly. I could show him the battle lines that run through America and the numbers that drive her politics. I understand it all, but he understands none of it.

But I don't do any of that.

Everyone needs to lose.

Soon, he'll lose. But perhaps he won't be embarrassed. He'll lose, but at least his eyes will be open and his conscious clear.

The Domestic Crisis

As I watch, Everyone is led out of the Candidates' soundproof room. He's the last of them. The other candidates had spent their time silently waiting for their opportunity. Occasionally, we broadcast a feed of them sitting, stoically – perhaps making notes on little paper notebooks. The hope, of course, is to capture a bit of nervousness; a bit of weakness in the face of the unknown.

But Everyone wasn't like them. Uncharacteristically, He spent his entire time talking to Rachel. It started with errata. He talked about her cat, about her favorite color. *She* was nervous at first, it was all being broadcast nationally. But she fell into a rhythm, eventually. And then he shifted the topics. He talked about where she'd come from and where she wanted to go. She was a smart and thoughtful woman.

Whenever we cut to the waiting room, the commentators were drawn to their conversation. There are only so many times you can comment on how stoic somebody is trying to be. However, as much as they tried, the commentators couldn't understand what Everyone was doing.

But I knew. I understood.

As the other Candidates prepared for combat – as they prepared to make the tough calls necessary to win – Everyone knew he wouldn't survive the coming battle. He didn't have what is needed. He wasn't realistic enough, not practical enough.

And he'd accepted that.

So, instead of focusing on the battle ahead, he was doing something *more* productive with his time. He was showcasing *Rachel* so that this day wouldn't be *her* last on the big stage.

It was a beautiful thing to watch.

As expected, the other candidates had done exactly what they'd needed to. Each in turn had been led out of the soundproof room. They'd taken their seat behind the massive replica desk in the faux Oval Office. And then a 'staffer' had rushed in with news.

"Mr. (or Mrs.) President," he'd announced breathlessly, "An unarmed black teenager has just been shot by the police."

The real politicians nailed the challenge. They'd asked all the questions necessary to seem even-handed. And then, one-by-one, they'd pandered to their base while trying not to say anything too offensive to the rest of country.

For some, the shooting was "an unfortunate accident in a high-stress situation," for others it was revealing of "a racism that we as a country still have to overcome." Some called for patience and trust in the local investigatory processes; others called for task forces designed to identify and ferret out hidden racism. And a few took more radical positions. One called (despite the lack of evidence provided by the staffer) for federal charges against the police. Another (again, despite a lack of evidence provided by the staffer) suggested the teenager had been a criminal and had somehow gotten what he had deserved.

Freddie came closest of all to satisfying everyone. He called for an investigation. But he also called for patience. His administration, he promised, would deal harshly but fairly with racism – even as it understood the challenges faced by the police. He announced an increase in funding for both community programs and police salaries. He tried, as well as one could, to make everybody happy.

It was a no-win situation; he couldn't have done better. An Emperor knows to distribute his favors and that's exactly what Freddie did.

But I knew Everyone wouldn't do that.

I knew he'd try something else, and he'd fail.

And he knew it too.

As Everyone – the last of the candidates – is led down the tunnel I see a martyr being led to his execution. Everybody watching knows what is about to happen.

He's a martyr, but also a flash in the pan. Soon enough, he'll be forgotten.

Everyone takes his seat. His eyes roam over the glass wall, almost frantically trying to see the faces watching him. Then he closes his eyes, intertwines his hands and closes his eyes.

Rachel is standing by his side.

His eyes are still closed when the staffer rushes in. And I can't take my eyes off of what I'm watching, even as I know that this is the end of Candidate Everyone.

School

"Mr. President," the staffer announces breathlessly, "An unarmed black teenager has just been shot by the police."

Everyone opens his eyes. He gets up from his desk, silently. Rachel and the staffer just watch him.

"I know," he says, facing the one-way glass, "That this is a fictional scenario. I know I'm supposed to be cold and calculating. I know I'm supposed to choose *which* Americans matter more to me. I know I'm supposed to pander to their priorities."

He stops and shakes his head. "The problem is, there's truth to this fiction."

He purses his lips and then continues, "I know *everybody* watching this has felt, at some point, imprisoned or trapped. Sometimes they have been constrained by forces none of us can control. But often we are imprisoned by *ourselves*. I know this to be true. I have lived it.

"That is why I can recognize that this 'fictional' scenario is one of those situations. In this moment, I can't know who was right or who was wrong. But *we've* created a prison for ourselves. Its walls are the relationships between black and blue and white and brown. They are made of fear, resentment and apprehension. We aren't the only ones with these walls. They exist in every society. But that doesn't mean we can't be free of this reality."

The other candidates are silent. The audience is silent. I imagine the nation is silent. Wondering where Everyone is going with his little speech.

"The question, of course, is how? Some want to bust out and kill the guards. They choose anger and resentment. But that only builds another, worse, prison. Anger and resentment have fueled catastrophic wars in Lebanon, Yugoslavia, the Congo, Syria and many other places.

"Others choose the path of redistribution, transferring money or assets from rich to poor or from white to black. They want to be the wardens. This may yield some rough form of *justice*, but it doesn't actually help them. Economic redistribution has undermined the economies of Venezuela and Zimbabwe. It has hurt everybody.

"I watched this all from my prison. I've seen people trapped and I've known what it's like. And I've known that there was nothing I could do. People were trapped, and there was nothing I could do."

He pauses, takes a breath.

"But now I *can* do something. At least in this fictional scenario, as President of the United States, I *can* do something. We are not powerless. We can break the prison of circumstance. And we can live free.

"As immigrants to this country have long shown, *education* provides an opportunity for the *next* generation to be stronger than the one that came before. And education is an area in which we have fundamentally failed the children of our inner cities.

"My idea is simple: let us provide transport and tuition grants to every student – from Kindergarten onwards.

"But not everybody will receive the same grant.

"Instead, students from lower-income families will receive grants that are greater than the median cost of education. And students from higher-income families will receive grants that are *smaller*. Larger grants will make lower-income students *more* desirable to educational providers, including those that have catered to wealthier families. Larger grants will give our poorest students access to the greatest advantage wealthier children have: access to quality education. When we raise people up, we can help prejudices gradually fall away. And, if you'll allow me a bit of poetry, we can use the walls of our prisons to build houses for our families.

"As with my healthcare initiative, parents can augment their grants with contributions of their own. Wealthier students will be able to attend the same schools as poorer ones – it will just cost more out of pocket. Nobody will be punished.

"And if parents don't spend the full grant amount they will be able to receive up to 5% back – in cash. Our educational costs have been spiraling upwards, without improving outcomes. So, just as with healthcare, we'll use the free market to improve *both* quality and cost. And with the 5% cap, parents will be prevented from cashing out on their own childrens' futures.

"Now, you might be worried this proposal will create other walls between us. After all, given the choice, the religious will go to religious schools, progressives to progressive schools, and African Americans to African American schools. Many who stand for public education argue that it can bring us together by fostering a single culture with a single set of values.

"But even if this worked, is a single culture *really* what we want? Don't we *want* to encourage a *diversity* of cultures? Won't *that* lead to a more vibrant and dynamic society? So instead of building a single house and making everybody live in it, why don't we just visit one another?

"It would be easy. We can randomly assign students to other schools within their geographic area for two weeks out of every year. Schools don't have to participate, we can't force anybody to do this. But we can make it a requirement if they want to be eligible for educational grants. We can require them both to host these 'ideological exchange students' and allow their own students to visit the schools of others. I imagine few will resist. And the students themselves will receive a small grant to encourage their attendance.

"In this way, the religious and the secular, the conservative and the liberal, the white and the Hispanic, the rich and the poor, the Jew and the Muslim can be exposed to one another as *people* even as they strengthen their own cultures. Through this, we can build a truly vibrant, diverse and *respectful* society.

"These sorts of shootings – these sorts of conflicts – aren't fiction. I'm afraid they never will be. But we can make things much much better. And we can stop throwing away so much human potential."

With that, Candidate Everyone turns and walks from the faux Oval Office. He heads down the tunnel towards the 11 Candidates who have been shocked by what they just heard.

I'm shocked. His campaign didn't die the death of a hopeless martyr. He didn't choose who mattered and who didn't. He didn't embarrass himself.

But I don't really know what he did do.

All I know is that Freddie won't be happy.

The Cloud

The next round of primaries were scheduled for the day after the show. After we'd wrapped up for the night, and once I'd had a chance to think about what Everyone had said, I realized just how stupid his statement was. He may not have used the words 'Redistribution', 'school choice', 'universal racism,' or 'reparations', but he implied them. And those are the catchphrases that fire up movements (and resistance to those same movements).

Candidate Everyone was basically begging for a universal upswell of condemnation from right, left and center. And that is what happened in the pundit class. As I watched that night and the next morning, I saw right-wing hosts attack him as a progressive and communist while left-wing hosts pegged him as a stool for the religious right. But I didn't see those messages on my social media. When people called into the shows or shared their own thoughts on Twitter or whatever, they seemed to say... "yes, but." As in, "Yes, he is the thing we can't stand, but..."

They were actually listening to what he had to say, rather than reacting before they could think.

Everyone's plans were full of holes. For example, education was primarily funded on the local level; a Federal program would have limited reach. Nonetheless, people were listening. And I began to think that they were listening *because* he was Everyone. He wasn't *yet* in anybody's box. He wasn't a Libtard or a right-wing slack-jawed idiot. He wasn't *yet* classified.

And so, people were able to hear what he was saying.

But hearing and acting are very different things. The fact is, as the polls open, nobody really knows what's going to happen. Who is his base? Who will be driven to come out and vote in a primary? How will he get the numbers he needs to get into the round of 8? These calculations are hard enough for a candidate with a clear political platform – but for Everyone?

Anything could happen to Everyone.

As noon passed, I thought about Everyone himself. He would be sitting in his hotel room; maybe watching those same empty-headed TV analysts. And even though Rachel would be there, I felt like he'd be alone. After all, Rachel is an employee. Or at least I think she is.

I think about when the actual votes came in. What then? If he did poorly couldn't he use someone to comfort him? And if he did well couldn't he use someone to celebrate with?

After all, he'd been alone for such a long time.

He shouldn't have to be any more.

About a half hour before the first primaries closed, I got in my car and I drove over to the Georgetown Hotel. I slipped through the lobby and I headed upstairs.

And here I am, standing outside his door, wondering whether I – the producer of the most important competition in the world – should really be visiting a contestant.

I hesitate for just a minute, and then – despite it all – I knock.

A moment later, the door opens. It's Rachel. She's smiling as she ushers me in. Once again, Everyone is sitting at the table. There are no papers on it. Everyone sees me and his face lights up. He jumps up from the table and walks straight towards me, his face plastered with a huge and unguarded smile.

"Amber," he says, "Thank you for coming."

In the background, a TV is playing. Some talking head is sharing his thoughts about Everyone, I'm sure of it. But Everyone isn't paying the TV any attention. The volume is too low to be heard at the table. I suppose Rachel is the one watching it.

"Hi," I say, "I thought maybe you two would like some company for the results?"

It sounds ridiculous. He's a Presidential candidate, he doesn't need me as friend.

Then again, nobody else is here.

"That'd be great!" says Rachel, "Should I order in some food?"

I don't want to bother Everyone with the bill. Room service can be so expensive. But then I realize he's running an actual campaign and quite a bit of money has been donated to it. And from what I've seen, they aren't spending it on anything *but* the hotel and room service.

"Sure," I say. With that, Rachel cheerfully gets on the phone.

I take a seat across from him at the table.

"This is all incredible," he says, "Unbelievable, really."

"What? That you might make it through another round?" I ask.

"No, no," he says, "That I am actually helping people."

He hasn't won anything, so I'm not sure what he means.

"Amber," he says, "I managed to tell *millions* of people about ways to make the world better. Me. Just a little while ago I was sitting in my basement. I'd never even *spoken* to another person in decades. And today? Even if I don't win, I've had the opportunity to make a difference."

His voice is confident, happy, proud.

"Thank you," he says, with a heartfelt smile.

I'm glad I helped him. I love how it makes me feel. Like I've done something really incredible myself.

As I look at him I realize that, cleaned up – and vibrant like he is – he *is* an attractive guy.

"What's it like?" I ask, "Suddenly having everybody watching you when, before, you were the one watching them?"

His expression flits through a shadow of his old worry. But then it clears and he says, "I don't know yet. I'm still getting used to the reality of it all, I guess. I can't actually *see* them watching me."

"Hm," I say. He has a point.

"What about Rachel and I, being here. Is it weird not to be alone?"

"It's, uh, it's harder to think."

"Oh," I say, "I'm sorry. Should, should we leave?"

"No, no, no," he says, "I didn't mean that. I mean, it *is* harder to think with *you* around. But, uh, in a good way."

His eyes fall back to the floor, like they did the first time we met. And he blushes. I suppose I do too.

Nobody has ever said anything like that to me before.

We just sit there, a little uncomfortable.

"Coffee?" Rachel calls out, her ear still to the phone.

I give her a thumbs up.

She orders a coffee.

Everyone looks back at me. I see a little of that fascination I saw in his basement the first time. But I see something else too. It's like a bit of him sees me as an *object*. I know the very idea is supposed to disturb me. But nobody's ever seen me as an *object* before.

I blush again.

I want to ask if Rachel is *also* a good distraction. She's quite pretty. So I ask, "Is Rachel also good to have around?"

Everyone nods, "Yes. She's very organized."

I nod. Is that the answer I wanted?

I think so.

We just sit there.

Rachel pipes up, "Foods ordered!"

Then she returns to the TV.

"What was your mother like?"

Everyone closes his eyes for a minute, thinking.

"I barely remember my mother," he says, "I barely remember what she looked like. We didn't have any photos around the house and year-by-year she just kind of faded away for me."

"Can you tell me anything?" I ask.

"I can," he says, "But just the facts. I mean, pretty much just the facts. I do remember that she loved me more than I can imagine any mother loving a child. I know that's saying a lot. But she did things for me that were incredible."

"Like locking you in a basement?"

"No, you have to understand *why* she did it."

"Why would any mother do that?" I ask.

"She wasn't normal," he answers, "My mother was... she was schizophrenic."

I just stare at him. For a moment I wonder whether he too is a little crazy.

"Schizophrenic?" I ask.

"Yes," he says, "I didn't know it when I was a kid. But she was. I worked it out later."

"So, did she think you were dangerous or something?"

"No, no," says Everyone, "Kind of the opposite, actually. It took me a long time to work it out – and more than a little bit of hacking – but my mother had a very specific and dominant illusion. She thought

95

she'd slept with a man and that man had the spirit of the *world* in him. She thought he was some kind of god. And she thought, literally, that *I* was some kind of angel. The offspring of Everything. That's why she named me the way she did. It's insane, I know. But I didn't know it then. She named me Everyone because I was the child of Everything."

I don't even know what to say.

Everyone just carries on.

"She had us registered with an address in Wyoming. I got a social security card and everything. But then she bought a very cheap house, with cash, in Detroit and we just disappeared. She didn't want anyone to know where Everyone lived. She thought there were forces in the world that would want to destroy me. And she thought I was too important to be destroyed. I had some kind of destiny to fulfill."

"And you believed her?" I ask.

"No... well... kind of. I did at first, of course. She was the only person I knew. And who doesn't want a destiny to fulfill. It was because I believed her that I stayed in that basement after she died. I was so torn up. I was in such pain. She was the only person I knew. Eventually, I just started trying to distract myself."

"By studying?"

"She thought I had a mission, a destiny. So, I did what I could to get ready for it. I read, I studied, I watched and I learned as much as I could possibly manage in that basement. But I forgot about the mission. The fact was I saw so much pain. I saw people's stories. I saw a world of people like me, suffering. I wanted to help them. Maybe, I thought, I'd figure out how to help me."

"But you were afraid?"

"But I was afraid. Eventually, I figured out my mom, that she was insane. But by then I'd been alone for so long that I was afraid to leave. I was freaking out when you actually knocked on my door. I didn't expect that."

He nods, pensively.

"Are you happy I showed up?"

He looks at me and then he says, with a warm smile, "I'm very happy you showed up."

I slip my hand towards his.

And he reciprocates, placing his hand gently over mine.

We just sit there, enjoying the moment.

A minute later, there's a knock on the door. And then a room service cart is wheeled in by a woman in a uniform. She pulls the shiny metal bells off the top of the food, places it on the table in front of me and then leaves.

Rachel has ordered me a feast.

As I'm about to start eating, she calls out, "The results are about to start coming in."

"Turn it up," I say. And she does.

I sit there, in Candidate Everyone's hotel room as the first state's results are announced. And they are stunning. Huge numbers of voters have turned out. And huge numbers have voted for Everyone.

Right out of the box, he's in the top two candidates. He'll need to be. The rounds are cumulative. To get to the top 8, he'll need to make up for his 2.3% showing in the first round of the competition.

I finish dinner as the results keep pouring in. I lay my hand back on the table and I smile when Everyone lays his hand back on top of mine. I drink my coffee. I watch. And I realize that he won't need comforting tonight. Celebration is in order.

My smile grows. Rachel jumps for joy with each new official announcement. She happy for Everyone, delighted even. But I know even she doesn't see the person *I* see.

And then, late into the night, it is done. Everyone came in second, behind Freddie. And he is safely in the top 8.

He's survived for another round.

Rachel gets up from her perch in front of the TV then. She gives Everyone a hug. And then she gives me one.

"I'm going home," she says. And then she looks at me with surprisingly mischievous eyes and says (with a wink), "Don't stay *too* late."

A minute later, she's gone.

I don't know what to do next. I've never been in this situation before. I decide to turn off the TV.

"I'll be right back," Everyone says.

He gets up and heads towards the bathroom.

I head towards the bar fridge in the little kitchenette. I open it. There's wine there. I grab a small bottle of wine, locate a corkscrew and get some glasses from the cupboard. I've just poured a glass for each of us when Everyone returns.

I watch him walk in, eager to see his expression. But I don't see what I want to see. Instead, I see anger and confusion and pain.

He holds his phone up and turns it towards me.

"Is this you?" he asks.

I look at the screen, confused. And then I see it. My conversation, my secure chat, with Freddie.

"I thought it would be good for ratings... I guarantee the weirdo is no threat... I will [finish the job]... the next round."

"Yes," reluctantly, "But–"

I want to tell him that *I didn't do it*. That 'the next round' is already done. That I only called him a weirdo because that's what would calm Freddie down.

But Everyone cuts me off.

"You were going to do it in the first round. When you told me to go into the weeds and not be personal." It is a statement, not a question.

I nod.

"But you changed your mind, for ratings."

"No," I insist.

"Bullsh-t," he says, "I should have known it was bullsh-t."

"It wasn't!" I insist.

But he doesn't seem to hear me. He seems to be collapsing in front of me. I see the torment in his angry face.

"My mother is right! I can't trust anybody."

"I can help you!" I say.

But he doesn't bother replying.

"I didn't do *anything*!" I insist.

He turns away.

"I *helped* you," I almost shout, "And you'll need *me* to get through this."

He turns back to me, for just an instant.

And he says, "I'm just a toy for you, a tool. You've already chosen who actually matters to you. And you've decided who's expendable."

Have I? Maybe the problem is that I haven't. I haven't been honest with Everyone.

I've still been hoping to take what Freddie has to offer.

I just watch him as he walks out of the living room and into the bedroom. I consider following him, pressing my case. But he won't hear me. I just stand there for a moment, stunned.

And suddenly, I'm crying.

I stumble through the suite's lounge, gathering up my things. And then I head for the door. I don't want Everyone to be alone. I don't want him to suffer. He doesn't deserve to suffer. But I have no idea what I could possibly say, or do, to make things better.

As I walk to the elevator, I get a text on my phone. I grab for it, eagerly. Maybe it's Everyone.

But it isn't.

Instead, it is a series of photos. Photos of me. Entering the hotel the first time. Scurrying through the lobby earlier this day. Sitting, with Everyone's hand on mine, just a few hours earlier. The room service waiter must have taken it.

And then there is the text. "The *Choose your Leader* trust has determined that you have been working with a Candidate in a biased manner. You are no longer the Producer of the show."

And just like that, I've lost Everyone and everything.

And I know that Freddie has orchestrated it all.

Nobody ever said that Muammar was a nice man.

I put the phone back in my pocket, step into the elevator and hit the button for the lobby. I plan on disappearing for a while.

But after a few moments, the doors open. Instead of the quiet lobby I'd walked through only hours before, the place is packed with reporters. A few security guards try hopelessly to push the crowd away. But there are too many and they are too eager. As cameras flash, and voices shout, I realize that Freddie isn't done yet.

Candidate Everyone has not yet been destroyed.

I hear the shouts.

"Did you help Everyone?"

"Did you tell him about the crisis in advance?"

"How long have you *really* known him?"

"Are you undermining our free process of elections?"

"Is Everyone corrupt too?"

I want to just say 'no comment' and walk away. I know that is the smart thing to do. But I can't. I can't let them destroy Everyone.

I hold up my hands. The room goes silent in an instant. My voice is shaking as I speak.

"I didn't give Candidate Everyone any information that was not already known to the other Candidates. I met Candidate Everyone during the 16th Candidate competition. I have not given him any inappropriate advantage over other Candidates. In fact, I believe Candidate Everyone's policies and actions should speak for themselves. America has voted for his innovative solutions and I think he deserves those votes. Candidate Everyone is perhaps the most honest and least corrupt person I have ever met in Washington D.C."

I stop for a second and a voice shouts out: "Are you sleeping with him?"

I just stand there stunned. I'm not going to answer that question. I shouldn't, should I? Would they believe a denial? I have to deny it, don't I? But I *want* to sleep with him.

What can I say?

I don't plan it. But I gesture towards my face, my impossibly ugly face, with my hands. Then I ask, through tears, "Would *anyone* want to sleep with me?"

I'm gesturing towards my face. But Everyone saw past my face, didn't he. *He* never seemed to notice it.

No, the problem now is that he seems to see the ugliness that is more than skin deep. The ugliness that *really* defines me.

The reporters are silent. They know they've gone too far. Nonetheless, I can hear the cameras flash. I push through them and over to the elevator that leads to the underground parking garage. I know *that* part of our exchange won't be on the news. Reporters don't like to make themselves look bad.

But things are bad enough even without that bit.

Thankfully, as the elevator doors open, the parking garage is empty.

Robotically, I step into my old Civic, start up the engine, and head towards home.

Aftermath

When I get home, I park on the street. There are reporters outside my small, Colonial-style house. I had the money for a bigger house when I bought it, but coming from Minneapolis the prices in D.C. blew me away. I just couldn't see paying for something larger (or for something even smaller in Georgetown itself).

Now, I regret it. I wouldn't mind a private driveway and a nice, fancy, gate – or even a doorman in a high-end apartment block. Sadly, those aren't among my options.

I push past the reporters, silently ignoring the barrage of questions and the flash of cameras. And then I shove my way into my house and I close the door behind me. The lights are off, but the place is lit up by the reporter's lights shining through the windows.

Any other night and the place would be silent. But tonight, I can hear them, outside. Milling around. trying to get shots of me through my windows.

I hear a helicopter hovering not too far away.

I walk from window to window, my feet creaking on the wooden floor. I imagine they can hear everything. I stand to the sides of the windows and I close the shades. And then I take a seat on one of the leather couches in my darkened living room.

I can't turn on the lights. After all, someone might snap a photo of me without me even knowing it.

I want to lay down and sleep, but I can't. I know they're out there. Perhaps some shady reporter will unlock a window and sneak in.

I don't want that.

I don't want any of this.

As I look around the room, helplessly, my eyes pass over the door to the basement. I don't know why, but it has a deadbolt, locked with a key.

I make my way to the kitchen drawer where all the random keys are kept. I fish around, and I find the one I want. And then I head back to the basement door.

I open it, I go through it, and I lock it behind me.

I turn on the light, a bright fluorescent. The walls are suddenly a gleaming white. And then I head down the old wooden staircase. With each step, I realize I am becoming more like Everyone, a prisoner in my own home, hiding from the world outside.

I get to the bottom of the stairs.

There's an old couch there, a crappy TV, a toilet and a washer and dryer. The floor is linoleum. I turn on the washing machine, to drown out the vestiges of the noise from outside.

Then I lay on the couch and, finally, fitfully, I fall asleep.

The next morning when I wake up, I can still hear the reporters outside.

I turn on the TV and I see my house. Somebody is droning on about something, but I don't want to know what. Then the picture shifts to Everyone's hotel. And I turn it up.

The fact is, as much as I want to hide, I want to know what's happening to *him*. But I learn only one thing: the hotel has driven the reporters out and they can't get anywhere near his room.

Stuck in my basement I can't really understand what is happening. And, as hard as I know the truth will be, I want to understand. I want to be aware. I gird myself and then dash upstairs, grab my laptop, and go back down to the basement.

I turn it on. I try to login to the *Choose your Leader* servers. I want access to our social media monitoring tools. But I'm locked out. Gradually, I realize that all I can do is sit here, watching the news; as generated and digested by other people. My slice of visibility into the real world – the world of individuals sharing their own thoughts – is just that: a slice.

Days pass. An independent board, selected by an auditing firm, takes over *Choose your Leader*. The reporters thin out. I order food in (one station covers its delivery). I watch the news obsessively.

Everyone drops in the polls. Voters report their distrust. Major media outlets report that *Choose your Leader*'s new board is considering banishing Candidate Everyone because of his collusion. Day after day, the coverage continues.

The slip in the polls is unabated.

And Everyone says nothing. Eventually, the press moves on. They can sense it, Everyone will end up being No One. The story isn't worth pushing. For its part, *Choose your Leader* still hasn't made a decision about Candidate Everyone. I wonder why? I wonder if, perhaps, Freddie no longer considers him a real threat.

When I'm not sufficiently distracted by the TV, I think about Everyone, hidden away in his hotel bedroom, ignoring the knocks on his door from the occasionally successful reporter. I imagine him forbidding room service from actually entering his room. I imagine his mother's paranoia taking over.

I can see the two of us just hiding from the world as it learns to forget us. We're separate. But in way, we've never been closer.

Then, one prime-time afternoon, somebody leaks the video of my final answer to the ambush at the hotel. My final pathetic response to "Are you sleeping with him?"

I want to curl up and die. I see the cruel responses on social media. I see the insults to my appearance. I see people calling me disgusting. One person claims Everyone only wanted me because I was the first person he'd seen, like a baby being imprinted by its mother.

I wonder if he's right.

I see even more people claim that I deserve everything I'm getting, and more. I'm corrupt. I'm vile. I'm filth.

I want to hide. I am hiding, but I want to hide more.

But then, within hours, I see the defenses. I see the messages of support. I see the arguments that women should not be judged by their appearance. I see my response being held up as *proof* of my truthfulness. I see people publicly calling on me, and Everyone, to push back – to fight back – to resist.

I see people calling on me to be strong.

The reporters come back to my house, hoping to see some sort of response from me. But I don't have it in me. I just stay in my basement.

Even if I was willing to face the press, I know I can't face off against Freddie. Not publicly. I couldn't possibly win. After all, there's a reason he's always been the face of our operation.

Eventually, the media's reporting turns back to *Choose your Leader's* pending decision on whether to ban Candidate Everyone. He's becoming a threat again. I can imagine Freddie secretly pushing whatever buttons he has at his disposal. But it doesn't go anywhere. Perhaps the new management realizes just how bad it would look for a company majority owned by one candidate to ban another.

At least my investment is doing well. Nothing is more talked about, nothing is more central, than the show. And I still own 20% of it.

Gradually, week by week, the next round of the competition draws closer. Finally, *Choose your Leader* announces that Candidate Everyone will *not* be banned.

In a public statement, the auditing firm itself states that while I *had* given Everyone pointers (I had been filmed doing so during the first round), that was my job. I was supposed to help make an ordinary citizen a valuable addition to the competition. In addition, I could not have known what the Domestic Crisis would be and so I could not have given Everyone any advanced information. Nonetheless, the *appearance* of impropriety also meant that the board will not be reinstating me. I will no longer be a producer on the show.

But, at least, Everyone will not be banned. Instead, he will be the fourth contestant in the most complex segment of the show.

The Foreign Emergency.

Foreign Emergency

When it came time to design segments for *Choose your Leader*, I went all in on the Foreign Emergency. After all, Candidates like to talk about their response to the 2am call, so we decided to show what that response would actually be.

The Foreign Emergency is just like the Domestic Crisis – in that it is a separation round. But there is a whole lot more involved. Just like with the Domestic Crisis, there is a critical situation and each candidate has to respond independently. But for the Foreign Emergency, we don't stop with an Oval Office and a staffer with a script. Instead, the Candidate is placed in a War Room staffed with make-believe military, intelligence and diplomatic staff. The Candidate is at the head of the room, with a video screen behind him that provides updates. It also provides a body count for the various parties involved.

Back-to-back from the War Room, but still visible to the audience, there is another room with an entire expert cast. That second room has 'representatives' from all the relevant nations and players in the scenario. Those representatives are actual experts in the countries or groups they playing in the simulation. For the purposes of the Foreign Emergency, they state what their own country/group's responses are to the actions of the Candidate in the War Room.

There is no representative for the American people, they are all watching.

Finally, there is a set of independent moderators who determine the outcomes of various activities. For example: if the U.S. takes a secret action, do the other players know about it? Or, if the two sides have a battle, what happens? Or, if the U.S. imposes sanctions, what does it do to the various economies?

In order to allow for secrecy, the other parties *type* in their responses, and the moderators share that which will be known to the President and the other players. The audience, of course, sees *everything*.

Put it all together and the 'President' can act in a realistic context. It is what the U.S. military calls a War Game. And, through this game, the American people can see how well the President would actually react to the 2am call.

Critically, this segment doesn't allow long speeches. Each Presidential action is limited to one minute with a total of five-minutes over the ten-minute segment. This challenge is about *action*, not words. In the first election, it moved pretty quickly.

One of the biggest benefits of the Foreign Emergency is the controversy it creates. If one candidate does poorly, they can easily blame another nation or player's representative (or the moderators) for being unrealistic. The result is a flurry of argument and discussion. We even encourage our own moderators and representatives to get involved on other media outlets. It all adds up to even better ratings for *Choose your Leader*.

It is a win-win situation.

That said, we don't *intentionally* stir up controversy. Instead, we assemble a set of experts from across the political spectrum and then, on the night of the show, we choose from them – randomly. This makes it hard to know the biases of the various parties, much less play off of them.

It is complex, but it works really well on TV. And, well, I love it.

Freddie, the primary vote leader so far, is first in this round. I don't have to be impartial anymore, so when Freddie steps into the War Room, I actually boo at the TV.

I'm hoping whatever challenge is planned (it is also kept secret by an accounting firm) will knock him off his feet.

Freddie, however, doesn't seem the least bit disturbed.

"What's happened?" he asks.

One of the Generals pipes up, "We got word that the Grand Ayatollah of Iran was assassinated by a Balochi suicide bomber."

Freddie turns to a diplomat, "Send our condolences to the nation and signal that we support them as they struggle to find the perpetrators."

The diplomat nods.

Then the General pipes up, "We now have word that Shiite paramilitary groups are attacking ethnically Balochi towns and villages in the southeast of the country."

The Balochi and Iranian body counts appear on the screen.

Freddie purses his lips. "Warn Iran that human rights abuses won't be tolerated."

In the other room, the Iranian representative types into his terminal. "Declare no human rights abuses, ignore the warning, terrorism must be punished."

A moderator forwards the comment to the War Room. He also places stock images of massacred villagers on the screen – for the American people to view. The body counts keep rising.

"What should we do?" asks the Diplomat.

"Send aid," says Freddie.

The Iranian representative types in "Secretly repurpose aid to support paramilitaries."

The moderator puts "Aid stolen" on the screen. There's a satellite feed of some vehicles intercepting a cargo truck somewhere in the desert. It is all very flashy.

The General pipes up, "What now Sir?"

Freddie thinks for a moment longer. "Apply sanctions against Iran."

The Iranian player responds, "Denounce sanctions. Explain we are just working against domestic terrorists."

The Russian, Pakistani and Indian players announce, "Ignore sanctions."

All the messages are put up on the screen. The moderator declares the sanction have limited economic effect.

"What now?" asks the General.

Freddie pauses for a long while. Then he says, "This isn't our conflict and, in recent cases, getting involved militarily has only created more problems."

Freddie turns to the diplomat, "Offer to host negotiations."

The Iranian player types, "Accept offer, but slow walk the negotiations and give nothing up."

Images of slaughter continue to play out on the screen. The body counts keep rising. Tens of thousands of Balochi and thousands of Iranians are dead. Another minute passes and then Freddie says, "Tell the American people that this blood is *not* on our hands. It was the decision of Iran to conduct these operations and its leadership will remain sanctioned until they are removed."

The slaughter doesn't stop. More minutes pass.

Finally, in the final minute of the ten-minute segment, the images come to an end. The body count stops rolling. And the Iranian player types: "Declare that the Balochi terrorists have been suppressed."

Then, with an almost relived face, Freddie walks off the stage.

He doesn't look good, but nobody is going to come out of this simulation smelling like roses. They can't do the standard games of distracting the public from the slaughter; that might work in real life but it would look awful here.

The next candidate up takes an entirely different approach. He issues threats. Then he declares that the U.S. has to live up to its promises. He bombs Iranian cities. The body count starts rising. Iran responds by bringing shipping in the Gulf to a halt with underwater mines and speedboats, starting the U.S. body count. Oil prices rise, European countries decry the American actions. The U.S. pushes forward. They are about to clear the Gulf when Russia – which has benefitted from high oil prices – gets involved. Their forces actually come to blows. The Russian body count starts and the U.S's keep rising. Then Iranian cruise missiles begin targeting Saudi, Kuwaiti and UAE oil fields as well as regional U.S. bases. Next, Hezbollah launches hundreds of thousands of missiles against Israeli cities and Hezbollah affiliates in Latin America start attacking U.S. interests there. Tens of thousands of Israelis die. Israel threatens nuclear conflict. Scenes of destruction play out on the screen. Finally, the U.S. overwhelms the combined Iranian and Russian militaries and occupies major Iranian cities. The body count slows, but keeps rising nonetheless. As time runs out, I realize that I'm seeing the end of a Candidate. That performance was catastrophic.

And all of Freddie's warning seem prophetic.

The third Candidate takes yet another approach. She implores Pakistan to step in. There are Baloch there. Pakistan agrees, in exchange for further military aid. But then they use the military aid to strengthen the border and crack down on Balochi activities. They want to contain the uprising and any Baloch calls for a homeland. The Candidate considers military force, but decides against it. She figures the Iranians have already achieved most of their objectives and so there'd be no point. She ends up in a spot very similar to Freddie's. Baloch casualties, but not many of them and stability returned to the region.

I hate to admit it, but Freddie has done a solid job. He may be a bastard, but I guess that's part of the job description. And, given his overall popularity, he is looking very very hard to beat.

And then I see Everyone walking down the tunnel.

He's frightened again. Alone.

I wish I could help him, somehow.

But I'm looking at a TV in my basement.

And all I can do is watch.

Chabahar

Everyone walks into the War Room. He's glum. His eyes dart around just as they used to.

One of the Generals pipes up, "We got word that the Grand Ayatollah of Iran was assassinated by a Balochi suicide bomber."

Everyone's eyes flit to him. "It's all a game isn't it?"

The General doesn't seem to notice. He continues with his script.

"We now have word that Shiite para-military groups are attacking ethnically Balochi towns and villages in the southeast of the country."

The death counter begins to move.

"It's all a damned game to you. A war game. But this isn't a game. There are real people suffering in real conflicts and all we seem to do is ignore them or make things worse."

The General looks confused for a moment. But he's paid to play a part. "So, what are you going to do about it?"

Candidate Everyone looks at him like he's crazy. He slumps into his chair. He grabs his hair in his hands. I think he's going to break, on national TV. But then his head pops up.

"Show me a map of the area."

The moderator does exactly what he says. Candidate Everyone stands up and points at a spot on the coast, within the Balochi region.

"There," he says, "The town of Chabahar near the Pakistani border. Send an expeditionary force there."

"Yes, Sir!" says the General. He's relieved to be back on script.

"There are women and children under fire. They're running. And they've got nowhere to go. We'll provide them a safe haven. U.S. forces will secure the city of Chabahar and welcome in refugees. No arms or fighters will be permitted and no operations against Iran will be permitted from within the City. We don't want war. We just need to give people temporary refuge during a dangerous time."

The Iranian representative in the other room types, "Denounce American invasion, mobilize forces to move against it."

Their move is presented on the War Room wall.

"Idiots," Everyone announces under his breath.

He thinks for a moment.

"Fine," he says, "Let's go further. Give the city free trade with the United States and let's do our best to give it a transparent legal system based on laws not favors. One that will help with economic and social development. Forget refuge, let's make this place the best place in the whole damned region to live in. Oh, and tell the Iranians if they come closer, they will regret it."

"Call their bluff," types the Iranian representative, "Move forces closer."

"They're moving forces closer," says the General.

Candidate Everyone actually smiles. "Really?"

"Yes..." says the General.

"Fine, let's play the game. Lots of Americans like lots of guns. They say they have them in order to defend freedom. Well, now's their chance. Let everybody know they can deposit working weapons at National Guard bases throughout the country. We'll take names and serial numbers so we know who owns what. If Iran persists, those weapons will be air dropped over opposition neighborhoods in major cities as well as Balochi and Kurdish regions of Iran. If Iranians want to be free, we'll give them the tools they need to get there. Or, the government can back the f-ck off."

I'm stunned by the language, but the moderator seems stunned by the action. He has to think for a long while before he types, "12 million guns donated."

The Iranian representative doesn't react initially. And then he types, "Withdraw forces."

It shows up on the board.

Candidate Everyone just watches the board. "They kept pushing, so let's stay in Chabahar. This city can be an example of what law, freedom and an alliance with the United States can do. We don't have to force freedom on anybody, but we can make it available to the people who really want it."

Iran does nothing. Russia's representative warns the U.S. not to try the same thing with them. But nobody else gets involved.

Before the time is even up, Candidate Everyone announces, "Return the guns."

And with that, he walks off the stage.

The moderator thinks and then types "Chabahar grows from 100,000 people to 1.3 million. It becomes a regional powerhouse."

With that, the scenario is over.

I just look at the screen, stunned. Everyone wasn't exactly the model of cool-headed decision making. He was angry, he was emotional. But he was damned effective. The death rate is far lower than even Freddie's. And the possibilities are far greater.

The rest of the Candidates cycle through. All follow one of the first three paths. None come close to what Everyone proposed.

Nonetheless, I could see his pain and I know that he needs me.

I sit there, in my basement, long after the show has ended. I watch the TV news, wondering if the reporters have come back and are hovering outside my house – waiting for some reaction from me.

"I won't give it to them," I tell myself. "I won't do anything."

But then I realize that I will. I realize that I must. I have to tell Candidate Everyone how proud I am of him. He has to know somebody cares about *him*.

I turn off the TV, climb the stairs and grab the keys to my car. I move as silently as I can, wondering if they have super-sensitive microphones trying to track my progress across the old wood floors. Leaving the lights off, I go to a side room and unlock a window. The *snick* of the mechanism sounds like gunshot. And then I tug at it. It jerks open with a *thuk*. I don't hear anything from outside. I crawl out of the window. I'm as quiet as I can be. I creep around to the back. There's a cameraman sitting on my lawn, watching the backdoor. I can't get past him; the place isn't that large. So, I head the other way. There's a news truck parked in front. As nonchalantly as I can manage, I walk straight down my driveway and towards my car.

It takes about five seconds for the reporters to see me. A flood of flashes unload as the cameramen kick in gear. They get shots of me unlocking my car, opening the door and getting in. I pull out of my spot and gun the engine, hoping to get outside of the range of their cameras.

But I know they'll be following me.

I race down the road and see the vans pull into the street behind me. Apparently, their drivers were ready for this. I could drive straight to the hotel, but I know I don't want them photographing me going there. Candidate Everyone doesn't need me photographed going there. And so I turn north instead, towards the Beltway. There are benefits to driving a gray Honda Civic – I should have an easier time than most when it comes time to disappear. But I know it won't be easy enough. As soon as my car shows up at the hotel, they'll have me again.

Then, I have another idea.

I head to Dulles Airport instead.

The news vans trail behind me as I patiently drive to the airport and park my car. They can't fit in the parking garage. I jump out of my car and race towards the terminal on foot. But instead of buying a ticket, I jump into the first car rental van I see. A few minutes later, we pull up to the car rental terminal. I get off the van and dash inside the building. It is almost deserted.

There's a woman behind the counter. She recognizes me immediately.

"Amanda Martin," she says, "How can I help?"

"I'm being followed by the news," I say. "I need something anonymous I can disappear with."

She nods.

"Okay," she says, "One gray Honda Civic coming up!"

"No, no," I say, "Not that!"

"Oh, don't worry," she says, tossing her head back towards a TV, "I was just joking. I just I saw you on TV. We don't actually have Hondas."

She turns her little terminal towards me and says, "But we do have Kias. You don't want to go too low end; it'll stick out at the Georgetown Hotel. Rent the littlest one we got and I'll bump you up – for free – to a mid-size SUV. You'll be as anonymous as you can be."

I give her a relieved smile, sign the form and hand over my credit card. Two minutes later I'm heading out the gate in an some kind of

Kia SUV. I drive to the hotel without incident, pull into the parking garage, slip through the lobby and before long I find myself standing outside Everyone's door.

Then, I just stop. What should I say? What can I say? I can't beg myself back into his good graces. He doesn't trust me, it's that simple. I suddenly realize, despite all the effort, that there's really no point in being here.

Then again, he is alone. He has Rachel, but really, he is alone. He might not trust me, but there's nobody *else* he can trust either.

I decide to do the best I can. I pull a slip of paper from my bag and I write:

"I hope you understand what has happened. And I want you to know that if you ever need me, I am here for you. I would be honored to help you."

I think about writing more, about explaining what has happened in detail. But I know that he has to come to that himself.

He's a smart man. He can work it out. He can figure out that I was supposed to destroy him, but didn't. Perhaps more importantly, he can figure out that *I* was destroyed because I didn't destroy him.

I sign the note, slip it under his door, and leave.

I go back to the airport and then back to my car. The press is gone; perhaps they think I took a flight somewhere. I get into my old Honda, smelling the familiar smells. And then I just start driving.

I don't know where I intended to go. But two days later, I pull up outside a single-story tract home on Myrtle Lane in plain vanilla Medicine Lake, Minnesota. The house has a few trees, a well-kept yard and a little flower patch outside the front door.

Otherwise, it would seem to be nothing special.

But it is something special.

Even before I turn engine the off, my mother is bustling out the front door. It is hard to imagine a woman as big as her being quite *that* agile. But she rushes towards me, her face split in two by a massive smile.

As I step out of the car, she caroms into me, reaches around me, and gives me exactly the kind of massive hug I didn't know I needed.

It's nice to be home.

Backroom Deal

"It's not a movie, mom!" I insist as she shoves a tub of buttered popcorn in front of me.

"Doesn't have to be," she says, with a smile. "Popcorn goes with anything."

A moment later, she cheerfully lowers herself onto the thick fabric couch. It has cupholders.

I just sigh and turn my attention to the TV.

I've been staying with my parents for weeks. I'm kind of surprised the press hasn't worked it out.

It's been nice though, being left alone.

As soon as I got into the house, with its hand-crocheted curtains, doilies and 3-inch pile carpets, my mom wanted to know why I was back. She honestly didn't know. But then she saw the look on my face and she said, "Man trouble?"

"Yeah," I answered.

"That bad?" she asked.

"Worse," I answered.

So, we sat down with a couple of cups of hot chocolate (with marshmallows) and we just talked. I told her everything. She knew none of it. Her own daughter was the producer on *the* biggest TV show there had ever been and she was satisfied just telling everybody about it. She'd never thought to actually watch it.

But she was delighted to sit there and listen. And listen she did. By the time my father came home from his job as a manager at an office supplies warehouse, we'd caught up on everything. She said 'hi' as my dad walked in the door. My dad looked up and saw me, and even though I hadn't been home in over a year he just kind of nodded and said, "Hey Amber."

Then he walked over the fridge and grabbed himself a beer.

My mom just beamed after him, smiling again from ear to ear. And then she turned back to me and said, "You know, Amber, you can stay as long as you need to."

And so that's what I did. For the first few days, I checked the election results incessantly. Candidate Everyone had shot to the top of the polls. In the round that followed the Foreign Emergency, he'd done far better than even Freddie had. Then my mom caught me checking my phone and she *actually confiscated it*.

"I need my phone!" I insisted.

"Why?"

"For work," I said.

"You don't have a job."

"I could get one!"

"You can wait," she said. And that was that.

So, I turned to the TV. Until she unplugged it too.

"That stuff isn't any good for you," was all the explanation she gave. And it was all the explanation I needed. She was right. But the whole situation began to feel a bit like I was in rehab, and being weaned off of something particularly addictive. Going cold turkey was hard, but I did it. And within a week I was just like her, enjoying myself in the house, working in the garden, and pretty much unaware of anything further away than the grocery store.

And I did enjoy her house. Sometimes people say a home looks like a woman lives in it. Well, my mom's home *was* that woman. It hugged you just like she did. It was warm and comforting. It always smelled of cookies or muffins or something else baking. And it put love far above any other considerations. It was easy to slip into its routine. I moved into my old bedroom at the end of the hall. And, some days, I didn't even get out of my pajamas.

I was exactly where I needed to be.

And then, about three weeks in, after my dad got home from work, my mother dragged us to the living room and plugged in the TV.

"What's going on?" I asked.

"Ah," she said, with a smile, "We're watching your show."

"What?!?" I said, suddenly a bit panicked. I didn't want to undo all my progress.

"The next episode, *The Backroom Deal*, is on tonight."

I had completely forgotten about it.

"Why do you want to watch the show?" I asked.

"Simple," she said, "I want to see the guy you've been moping about."

So that's where I am now.

We've got huge bowls of popcorn. Cans of coke and beer. Even some chips and salsa. My dad is in his La-Z-Boy and my mom and I are sitting back in that incredible cushy couch (also a La-Z-Boy). And we're just waiting.

The Backroom Deal starts in three minutes.

I'd never seen the show this way, as a total outsider. It is exciting to watch the opening sequence and then the host walking through the scenario.

"Welcome America!" he declares, "To another Episode of *Choose your Leader*!"

The crowd in the arena bursts into applause.

"We are down to the final four candidates!"

More cheering. The host signals with his hands, quieting everybody down.

"Now this week's segment is different than before. This week, the Candidates go head-to-head in a group activity. On a bare stage, they have to hash out an agreement. And we get to see just how well they can negotiate on our behalf!"

More cheering.

"We all know politicians will actually negotiate by trading on their own personal priorities and those of other politicians. They'll trade favors. Of course, they won't do that here, it wouldn't look good. But they will trade *their* voters' priorities against the priorities of the other Candidates. This is our chance to see just how much they'll have to sacrifice to get what their supporters really want."

Cheering again.

And then, to a massive rush of applause, the Candidates walk onto the stage. The stage is truly simple this time. There's a main area and two little rooms (all three are set up with microphones and video recording equipment). The concept is straightforward. All four candidates can negotiate on the main stage – or they can break off to discuss things on the side using the small rooms.

They all line up, the four of them, facing the host. Everyone is a step behind the others. He doesn't look confident.

"Which one is he?" asks my mom.

I point, "The guy with the glasses."

"Okay," she says.

The host pulls an envelope from his pocket.

"Candidates," he says, "Our auditing firm has created today's scenario. Nobody, outside of that firm, has seen it until tonight. I'm going to tear open this sealed envelope and read the scenario to you. Are you ready?"

The Candidates nod. The host tears open the envelope. Then he pulls out a single folded white sheet of paper.

He unfolds it and begins to read:

"Candidates," he says, "There's has been an economic slowdown. Unemployment has gone up while tax receipts have gone down. More and more people are out of a job. You, the politicians, have to work out what to do."

He pauses and then asks, "Do you understand?"

All four Candidates nod.

"Then have it!" says the host. A moment later, he retreats to the side of the stage.

Freddie and Everyone don't say anything at first. Instead, the other two candidates announce their starting positions. One is an economic conservative, the other a liberal. One calls for income tax cuts to stimulate the economy while the other prioritizes greater aid for those left out of work by the slow down.

They hem and haw, going back and forth but really getting no closer together. Everyone just watches them.

Then Freddie speaks up, "Folks, the American people need help. They need a resolution. They don't need us arguing and not doing what needs to be done. So, let's work something out to make things better."

In a sentence, Freddie has captured the essence of the round. It is to negotiate; it is to bring people together. And without taking any position of his own, he'll make it look like *he's* the one who can get things done. I realize in that moment that I know *who* he is. He's Candidate No One. He has no position and stands with nobody.

It's a very good place for politician to be.

As the other two candidates consider their positions, I see Everyone close his eyes. His jaw is set in frustration. I feel myself trying to anticipate what he's going to say. But, of course, I can't.

The right and the left get back to arguing. They can't surrender their positions just because Freddie asked nicely.

Then, Everyone speaks.

"Can't you guys just see the tradeoff? If you don't help the poor, they suffer. And if you help them too much, they won't need to work, slowing down the economic recovery."

The left-wing guy jumps in, "Welfare and unemployment are never enough to stop people from working."

The right-wing guy almost jumps on top of him, "Poor people suffer the most when the economy sucks. We just need to get it back on track."

Candidate Everyone looks at the two of them.

"People are suffering, they aren't living up to their potential, and that's all you've got?"

Surprisingly, Freddie jumps in, "I think we should hear what Everyone has to say. He might be able to help."

The other two Candidates shoot death stares at Freddie, but they quiet down. I know, in my gut, that they should be thanking him.

I *know* this is some kind of trap.

"We all want people to work, right?" Candidate Everyone says.

"Yes," the other three agree.

"So, let's do that. Let's get rid of the minimum wage so almost nobody is priced out of the job market."

The left-wing Candidate begins to spool up but Freddie puts his hand on his shoulder and encourages him to wait.

"There's more, I hope," Freddie says to Everyone.

"Yes, of course," says Everyone, "If workers have the wrong skills for a changing market place they shouldn't find themselves on unemployment. Instead, they should work and the *government* should subsidize their income. It should give their lower incomes more spending power to make up for their low wages."

"How?" asks Freddie.

"Simple," says Everyone, "A progressive sales tax."

"What?" asks Freddie, showing a touch of confusion.

"We can track individual spending, electronically. So, let's have a national sales tax. But then, to avoid hurting the poor, let's have it start off as a negative tax each month. So, you might buy something for $100, but only pay $10 after tax. As you spend more, this subsidy will go away until it becomes a tax. This setup will mean that those who have few skills – or the wrong skills – can still work. They won't be paid much, but their money will go far. Most importantly, they'll be able to experience the fulfillment of work and not be locked out by their limited economic worth."

The others look at him, thinking about it.

Everyone continues, "This tax can replace *all other taxes and welfare*. We'll get rid of income tax, payroll taxes, corporate taxes, complex welfare benefits and all the rest. We'll streamline everything, providing a boon to the economy (except for accountants) even as we move towards maximum employment."

The others have had a chance to think now.

"What about business expenses?" asks the right-wing candidate, a touch of aggression in his voice.

"We can make business purchases and charitable donations tax free," says Everyone, "And if you buy a major asset that's not a business expense – like a house or a car – you'll be able to get back some or all of the tax you paid when you sell that asset to the next person."

I see the other candidates thinking, trying to formulate their responses. They want to attack; they need to attack. But they aren't quite sure how.

The right-wing candidate says, "This isn't easy to implement."

"We'll have to be inventive," says Everyone, "But credit and debit cards are already linked to individuals. Businesses already collect sales tax. And people, especially poor people, would be eager to participate in the system."

"Well, at first glance," says the right-wing candidate, "I have to say this sounds like you'd be helping the poor while getting people into the work place and cutting red tape for everyone. It sounds like a pretty good recipe to fix the problem we're facing."

The left-wing candidate asks, "What about those who *can't* work."

"Charities can provide them with money. And that money's spending power can be boosted, just like with any other initial monthly spending."

Everyone has clearly thought about this.

He nods and asks, "And families?" he asks.

"A family would just pool their subsidy. A couple married with two children would have four times as much negative tax available as a single individual. Anybody could pool subsidies, not just families."

They all stop and ponder for a moment. Then, Freddie jumps in and I know the trap is about to be sprung.

"You want to encourage work?" he asks Everyone.

"Yes," says Everyone.

"You think it's important for people to experience the fulfillment of productive activity."

"Yes," says Everyone.

"Hm," says Freddie, his eyes flashing, "And are you an example of this sort of living?"

"What?" asks Everyone, a dash of fear crossing his face.

"Well, let's see," says Freddie, "You are preaching to the nation about getting people into the workforce. But you've never had a job, have you?"

"Well, no," says Everyone.

"In fact," says Freddie, "You've lived you whole life in your mother's basement."

"Yes, but everybody watching knows that," says Everyone.

"I know," says Freddie, "But do they know how you paid for it?"

Everyone's face goes suddenly pale.

"Folks," says Freddie, turning to face the crowd, "Candidate Everyone wants to pitch us on his crazy ideas for rebuilding the United States from the foundations up. But I think you need to know who you're dealing with. Did you know Candidate Everyone here has been living off his mother's long-term disability insurance? Did you know she died *25 years ago*! He buried her in the backyard, but he never reported her death. He just kept *stealing* from the insurance company. He's a fraud and he's never worked a day in his life. His schemes are crazy. And I think we should all be very very wary of what he proposes."

Everyone just stands there. I wish I could jump into the TV and defend Everyone. Freddie's only sharing a part of the story. Everyone's was only a kid when his mom died. And it isn't so easy to get out in the world. But Freddie's no idiot, he's sprung this at exactly the right time. And he'd tear Everyone apart at any sign of weakness.

Candidate Everyone physically pulls away from the center of the conversation. The other Candidates just stare at him, admonishing him with their eyes.

It's great TV.

Of course, they also all benefit by taking Everyone off the board.

"What should we do?" asks the left-wing Candidate.

"I propose a commission of qualified economists to study Everyone's proposal," says Freddie, suddenly sounding generous. "But in the meantime, let's use more convention tools."

And that's what they do. While claiming everything is temporary, they cut taxes, increase spending and fund it all with debt.

Everyone doesn't say another word.

And then, before I can get over my shock, the episode is over.

My mom looks at me. "So," she says, "You're telling me all this trouble is over *that* man?"

"What do you mean, mom?" I ask, defensively.

"Amber," she says, "You are, or were, the producer of the biggest TV show on planet Earth. You've helped reinvent our entire political system. You've made millions – maybe tens or hundreds of millions – and you're going to all this trouble over *that* man?"

I just look at her, confused.

"Amber," she says, "He's a loser who lives in his dead mother's basement and wouldn't know how to dress himself without your help."

I just stare at her.

"Amber, Amber," she insists, "You could do a hell of a lot better than *that* man."

From his Lay-Z-Boy I hear my father grunt his agreement.

And I begin to wonder.

Do *I* only want him because he's the first man who seemed to want me?

I want to argue with my parents. I want to insist that he's better than he looked in that contest. But I don't know what to say. Maybe they're right, maybe I do just have to get over him.

Slowly, I get up off the couch and pad my way to my room through the thick carpeting. I lay down on my childhood bed, close my eyes and just hope that the confusion that seems to be overwhelming me will somehow sort itself out.

Vote

It doesn't sort itself out.

Instead, the next day, I find myself pulling on a hoodie (to hide my face) and sneaking out to watch the results. Amazingly, most of the TVs in the sports bars are following *this* story. I've managed to finally make politics a real spectator sport. And the spectators seem to agree: Everyone's chances aren't looking good.

The field is about to shrink from 4 Candidates to 2. With his performance in *the Backroom Deal* it looks likely that Candidate Everyone won't be one of them. In polling about the candidates, Everyone is faulted for being too inexperienced, hypocritical and dishonest. It is a heck of a list of charges for *Freddie* to lay at the feet of anyone else. But he's done it. And on top of it all, voters have begun to see Everyone as just a little too weird. The original story, the original plot line, has been brought back to life.

As I see the projections and the forecasts, I wonder whether I really did make the right choice. After all, I helped Everyone out. But despite that, he was taken apart by Freddie. And if I hadn't helped? Well – instead of watching polls in a sports bar in Minneapolis, I'd be planning the post-election Presidential agenda.

I could have mattered. I could have made a difference. Instead, I burned it all down for a man my mother thinks is a loser.

Eventually, the actual polls close and the results begin to post. As expected, Candidate Everyone is being trounced. He wins no states. In fact, he comes in a distant fourth in every one. I suck down a beer, absent-mindedly, with every new and mind-boggling bad result. Everyone is being destroyed. Everyone has been destroyed.

I begin to wonder if his flash in the pan will have any impact on American politics. There's a more likely result, of course. Whoever wins this election and the next one could simple "propose a commission of qualified individuals to study Everyone's proposals while in the meantime using more convention tools."

Everything Candidate Everyone stood for would be sidelined and the classic politicians could go back to fighting from the hilltops they already know so well.

It's 2am when I finally head home, in an Uber. I'm far too drunk to drive. There's was an outside chance Everyone could have slipped in. He did so well in the third round that his totals – over the prior three rounds – could have carried him into the fourth. Unfortunately, his numbers weren't even good enough to clear that low bar.

I stumble into the house. But I don't make it to my bedroom. Instead, I pass out on the couch. No man. No job. No future. Just a bunch of money that I don't really know how to spend.

I reassure myself, in my fuzzy head, that I'll find something to do with it in the morning.

And then I pass out.

When I wake up, my head is killing me. My mom is sitting on the chair opposite mine. She looks worried.

"You okay?" she asks, gently.

"Sure," I say, "Just dandy."

I pull my head off the slightly damp fabric of the couch.

Not pleasant.

She nods. She knows what's up. For all her buttery joy, she's not a stupid woman.

I expect her to say something like "you'll find something better" or "you'll land on your feet" or "you'll make it all work out somehow."

But she doesn't. She just looks at me thoughtfully and asks, "Do you think he can pull it off?"

"What?" I ask.

"Well," she says, "I put some money down with my bookie on Everyone being elected President. I mean, after everything you told me how couldn't I, right? So, do you think he can pull it off?"

"You have a bookie?!?" I ask, my head clearing just a bit.

"Yeah," she says, nonchalantly, "I like to bet on the Hockey, so..."

"How much did you bet?" I ask.

"A lot," she says, with a smile.

"When?" I ask.

"The night you came home," she says.

I just look at her. I want to cry; this is just adding insult to injury.

"Mom," I say, "He lost last night." I want to go back to sleep. My dreams were unpleasant, but at least they weren't real.

"Oh, no, he didn't lose last night," she says, with a bright smile.

"Mom," I say, patiently, "I watched it all. I was up until 2."

"You think you did," she said, "But I've been listening to the radio and, well, there were a whole lot of absentee and military ballots for this particular primary. Apparently, diplomats and soldiers liked what he did with the Foreign Emergency. And they voted *before The Backroom Deal*. And, so..."

I sit up suddenly and then grab my head in pain.

"Is he through?" I ask.

"I, I, don't know," says my mother, "But we can listen and find out."

And so that's what we do. We plop down in the kitchen, hot cocoas in hand, and we listen. It seems amazingly old fashioned, but it's what we do. Every news and talk radio station seem to covering the ballot.

Hours pass. And Everyone is getting closer and closer to the line. 1,000 votes were needed. Then 500. Then 200. Then, in one sudden burst, he is over the line. There will be recounts of course, but it looks like Everyone is going to make it to the final.

As soon as that is clear, the controversy explodes. The question is simple: if absentee voters didn't get to see his last performance before voting, should their votes count as far as the show is concerned? Does he actually deserve to get to the next round?

I want to call in to the shows. I know I could. One mention of my name and they'd put me on the air. But I don't have anything I want to share. After all, I know that if I were Freddie I'd be delighted with Everyone getting into the final this way. The rules are the rules, the controversy is *great* for business. People will tune in just to watch Everyone crash and burn. And, of course, any of the other candidates would also be destroyed by Freddie – so the #2 slot doesn't really matter, does it?

But I don't want to say any of that. I don't want to *say* that Everyone is going to lose to Freddie. I don't want to *say* that that result is inevitable. And I don't want to consider what it says about us as a people or what it says about the system I helped build. It is all just too damned depressing.

So, I listen. But I don't speak. And eventually, I just turn off the radio.

I imagine myself in Everyone's shoes, sneaking through into the final round. I imagine how bad he must feel. He isn't trying to take advantage of anybody. And, for a little while, I imagine that perhaps he's decided that the right thing to do is give his spot to another. Perhaps, just maybe, he'll leave D.C. Perhaps, just maybe, Rachel will drive him to Minneapolis. And perhaps, just maybe, we can buy a little house, unplug the TV, and live in our own little world.

Perhaps, just maybe, that's what Everyone would like.

It would all start with a text, right? I steal my phone back from my mother. I turn the ringer way up. And I wait, hoping to hear a familiar *Bing*. But nothing comes. Days pass and then I think that, perhaps, just maybe, he's decided not to text but just to show up and surprise me.

Then weeks pass and nobody knocks on the door.

The truth is inescapable.

He doesn't want me.

He'd rather give it all one last shot.

The Final

We're in the living room again. But there's no popcorn this time. No beer. No snacks. Instead my parents are sitting together on the couch and I'm on the floor, eyes close up to the TV like some kid from an old movie. This is the *Final Round*; just before the general national election. And Freddie Samuels is about to do what he does, close the deal.

The Final Round is the simplest of all of them. Two candidates. Each makes a prepared statement in front of a live audience. There is no moderator, no interviewer and basically no set to speak of. Just a wooden lectern and two wooden chairs off to the side of the stage for the candidates to sit on.

Walking formally, the host steps up to the lectern. He leans forward, toward the cameras, like he's about to share something important and a bit confidential. It's way acted.

He announces, "This is the Final Round. The last chance for the Candidates to make their case before *you*, our national TV audience. The leader, by votes counted, is Freddie Samuels. He will speak first."

The crowd is silent as Freddie and the host exchange places. The host heads for the chair Freddie just vacated and Freddie heads for the lectern. Candidate Everyone just sits there, waiting to see what Freddie will say.

As Freddie steps to the lectern, he smiles broadly. And then he begins to speak. "When I started this competition four years ago, I thought of it as a way to share ideas across party lines. I thought of it as a way to enrich the American people's understanding of the people they elect. But most of all, I thought of it as a way to bring people together. After the first election, in which America was split in two, I realized that something more than a *format* was needed to knit our country back together. As I toured on the 16th Candidate, I realized that an individual was needed. A uniter. Someone who could reconnect people – across party lines – within our communities, our cities, our states and our great nation. And then, with the advice of others, I realized that someone might be me."

I just watch, stunned at how smoothly Freddie recasts the past.

"I stand here, one of two remaining candidates. Both of us, in our way, are uniters. And our presence here is a testament to what is possible. But we are, the two of us, very different people. Candidate Everyone is unstable. Candidate Everyone is surrounded by scandal. Candidate Everyone has *never* competed in an election, or even held a job. And Candidate Everyone's very isolation has led to the development of his radical and generally unworkable ideas. We saw the cost of his isolation in *The Backroom Negotiation*. He didn't know how to engage with others and he didn't have enough respect for those who have built the system we have."

I wonder what else Freddie can do to destroy Everyone. The answer is 'plenty'. He continues, "All that said, I believe Candidate Everyone has a lot to offer. He needs to learn, but I believe he *can* help this country. I know many Americans find his ideas appealing. And I can understand why. So, if you elect me, I will make Candidate Everyone my Special Policy Advisor. I will give him the budget to explore and flesh out the concepts he has. And we, the American people, will adopt the best of what he has to offer without putting him in a position that he is unsuited for."

"That is my proposition, to you today. Vote for me and you will *also* be voting for Candidate Everyone."

I can't help but smile in horror at the audacity of Freddie's move. Everyone hasn't just been crushed, he's been *co-opted*. Freddie will manage him like he'll manage everybody else. 'Special Policy Advisor' is a meaningless and powerless position. The sheer political genius of this move is incredible. If he keeps this up, Freddie could probably secure as many Presidential terms as he wants.

And Everyone seems to have even less of a chance than he did just a few minutes before.

With that brief speech, Freddie heads back to the seats and Candidate Everyone gets up. Everyone walks almost casually to the lectern. It is as if he doesn't know he's about to address tens of millions of people.

When he gets there, he isn't smiling. But he doesn't look afraid.

He just seems like he's getting ready for an ordinary conversation.

I know it's an act, but I'm glad that at least he's trying.

Concession

As Everyone steps to the microphone, he begins to speak in a simple, conversation voice.

"My mother was sick when I was a child. She didn't just have cancer; she was schizophrenic. She raised me, in the basement of our home, because she was convinced that the world was a dangerous place for me. When she died, I buried her in the backyard and I didn't report her death. I continued to receive her benefits because I thought there was no other way to survive. The world was too dangerous a place, I *had* to stay home. As I got older, the idea of stepping outside of that house – of talking to people – just became more and more frightening. And so, I stayed there, far longer than I should have.

"Through that ongoing decision, or lack of decision, I committed fraud. I not only cheated others, I cheated myself. I failed to engage with the world. I failed to learn about people. I failed to contribute to the world. And I failed to grow. Freddie has only made the truth obvious to the world.

"I am a hypocrite. I am happy to speak about the redeeming value of work, but I have never worked. I am happy to speak about the redeeming value of social interaction, but I ran from it for decades. The fact is, I continue to speak to ideals that are far beyond my own actions. I will continue to be a hypocrite, because I believe *you* can all be a better example than I have been.

"I am not telling you this because I want *your* forgiveness. I'm not really speaking to America. I'm telling you this because I want Amber Martin's forgiveness—" my breath caught suddenly at the mention of my name "—You see, it was Amber Martin who got me unstuck. It was Amber Martin who came to my home and who was willing to step inside of it. It was Amber Martin who did what was necessary to help me push past my fear. That was Amber's job. Not because she was colluding with me, but because she was *supposed* to be making me ready for this show."

I was mesmerized. I was in the center of it all, and that wasn't even what I cared about.

"But, you see, Amber did *too good* a job. I know somebody else offered her a senior position if she set me up to fail. But she *didn't* set me up. And because of it, she was fired and embarrassed. She treated me fairly. And then, when I could have used her the most – when she could have rescued me from my own mistakes – *I* drove her away. I thought she was colluding *against* me.

"The fact is, I'm not very good at politics. I don't see the twists and the turns. I sometimes care too much to be impartial. And I don't know who to trust. When Amber was being honest and straightforward, I thought she was being deceitful. And when others were being deceitful, I thought they were being honest.

"Because of this, I will understand when you vote for Freddie Samuels. Because of this, I will gratefully accept the opportunity to serve as his Special Policy Advisor. I want to help. That's why I'm here. I want to help people do more with their lives. As part of that, I *will* learn from my mistakes. I know now that I must surround myself with people who know *how* to play this game; but who will take the higher road when the time for tough decisions comes. In my new position, I will surround myself with experienced people, people with the smarts to play this game – but also people of integrity. People like Amber, if she'll forgive me. If she'll forgive me, I'd like her help to find them. I'd like her to be my Chief of Staff.

"G-d Bless America."

146

With that, Candidate Everyone turns and walks from the stage.

The show breaks for an ad. I know what comes afterwards – a full season summary, reviews of dramatic moments and so on and so forth. I don't need to watch any of it.

I turn back towards my mom. I am about to tell her "I need to go." But she is already ahead of me.

In one hand, she has my car keys and purse. In the other is a plastic shopping bag filled to the brim with a stack of Tupperware containers. I know they contain ready-made-meals – it's what she always packs for road trips. And on the floor next to her is a small overnight bag.

"When did you do that?" I ask.

"Oh, last night."

"Why?" I ask.

"Because," she says, "I thought you might need it."

I leap up from the floor (well, as quickly as I can). I give my mom a hug and my dad a kiss (on his forehead). Then I grab the stuff and I charge through the door.

A minute later, I'm in my old Civic and racing towards D.C.

But not everything is answered.

Does everyone *only* want me as a Chief of Staff?

Or is there, perhaps, maybe, something more.

The Drive

I flip on the radio as I drive. *All* the coverage is about the show. Everybody is talking. At first, the responses are exactly what you'd expect. Freddie nailed it. Freddie hit it out of the park. A vote for Freddie is a vote for the best of both worlds.

But then the conspiracies begin appear in the cracks.

'Who, exactly, set Amber up? Who got her fired?'

As they pull at that thread, it comes out that the majority owner of the show *is* Freddie.

'Perhaps he orchestrated the whole thing.'

Some are impressed with the idea that he could pull that off. But not the kind of impressed that leads them to vote for a guy. Right and left the broadcasters begin to flirt with the idea that vote for Freddie might *not* be a vote for the best of both worlds.

Then one of the hosts announces, "*I've just received something remarkable from an extremely reliable source. It is a transcript of a chat.*"

The radio host then starts to read it. As soon as he does, I realize he has the Sanussi chat. The whole thing.

I imagine Rachel emailing from the hotel bathroom.

After he finishes, the host says, "*According to the source, 'Muammar' is a code name for Freddie Samuels. And 'Sanussi' is one for Amber Martin.*"

"*Muammar?* the talking head asks, "*Who does this guy think he is? And why did he pick that name?*"

The news of the memo travels from station to station. I imagine is doing the same thing on social media. And then, bit by bit, callers begin to suggest something different.

"Why not vote for Everyone?"

He can plug his leaks. He can make up for his mistakes. And, fraud aside, he's an upstanding guy. Freddie swings into action then. He calls into show after show. He denies any of the allegations. He laughs at the Muammar texts as an obvious fabrication. And he sounds so credible. After he gets off one particularly popular show, my phone rings.

I don't know the number, but I flip off the radio and answer it on speaker.

"Yes?" I ask.

I hear Freddie on the other end.

"Sanussi?" he says, in a hushed voice.

I can't imagine what he wants. But I don't care.

"Freddie," I say, "I have no idea what you want, but you oughtta know we're done with all that."

I hang up the phone.

And then, a minute later, I hear one of the talk show hosts intone:

"Folks, one of our number, a Freddie impressionist, just called Amber Martin's private cell phone. We gave her no warning. Here's what went down."

The call is played back and then transferred from station to station. Right wing to left, it is used to validate the memo.

In that moment, Freddie's credibility is crushed.

Then one show does some seriously quick research. They call the owner of the coffee shop I used to work for. And then they call former staff members of *Choose your Leader*. They interview them on the air. They ask about me. And the reviews are glowing. I ran the place. I made it happen. I loved working with the crew. I cared about them. I'm a stand-up person.

And, most critically, Freddie was just a talking head.

One staffer even tells about a time that he joked about being Muammar because he could *force* all the parties to work together.

My phone begins to ring. I don't know the numbers. I turn it off.

At 3am, I stop at a motel on the outskirts of Chicago. My life is playing out like a national soap opera. While the storyline would be great, there's no point in adding to it by dying just cause I'm in a rush to get back to Candidate Everyone.

I wake up 6 hours later. I use the hotel Wifi to load the route for the rest of the drive. I'm being flooded with emails and texts.

Then, airline mode on, I hit the road again. I flip the radio on and I realize that what was conspiracy the night before has turned to fact. Just like that, right and left, the outsider candidate has become the *preferred* candidate.

"*Vote Everyone,*" I hear on station after station.

But I have no idea if anyone is going to do it. After all, only political junkies listen to this kind of news. But, maybe political junkies will be enough.

I look at my ETA. The first polls will close an hour and a half before I get to D.C. The result might be known, one way or another, by the time I get to the Georgetown Hotel.

I drive and drive, listening the whole way. As I come closer, the first results begin to come in. Everyone is crushing the polls. I keep driving, hearing more and more. He's racking up state after state. I get to D.C. As I get close to the Georgetown Hotel, the streets fill with more and more people. It's almost impossible to drive.

Everybody seems to be walking towards the Hotel.

I try beeping and one woman looks over her shoulder, almost annoyed at the interruption.

And then she sees my face.

She says something to her friend, who says something to the next person and the next and the next. People see me and wave. They give encouraging whacks to the car. They flash me thumbs up. And they clear the way. The crowd splits in front of me like the Red Sea before the Jewish people. And I creep forward; carried forward by a wave of personal human communication.

Eventually, I reach the hotel. The Secret Service are there now. The results are not yet final. I pull up to the outside of the building and reluctantly turn off the car – and my radio.

The agents recognize me, but they check my ID nonetheless. And then I pass through their cordon.

I pass through security layer after security layer. The hotel is abuzz with excitement. Everybody knows Everyone is staying here. And, then, eventually, I get to Everyone's hallway. And he's standing there, right outside his door. He's got a cup of coffee in his hand and he's talking to one of the agents.

He glances in my direction and a huge smile breaks out on his face. He hands his cup to the agent, and rushes towards me. But he draws himself up just short of where I am.

"I'm so happy you're here," he says.

Suddenly the smile vanishes, like he's remembered something, and he asks, "Can you forgive me?"

Just then, the crowd outside erupts in cheers.

I answer, "Mr. President-Elect... you're forgiven."

The smile returns. And then he says, "I think you still owe me a glass of wine."

Epilogue

Our nation is divided into two fundamental camps. One camp (the right) emphasizes production, while the other (the left) emphasizes the absence of fear. This is most obvious in economic matters, but when you think about it, even the culture wars reflect this divide.

This contrast isn't new. It is as old the Bible itself. Adam doesn't create in the Garden of Eden. He has the absence of fear, but that isn't enough. He is driven out of it so that he will be productive and follow in the footsteps of G-d the Creator. It is better to have good and evil, creation and loss, than it is to have neither. Nonetheless, the world of risk and fear into which he is thrust is an imperfect one. And it becomes our mission to overcome loss, fear and evil. Looked at this way, the story of the Bible is about enabling the aspirations of *both* the right and the left.

But we don't seem to do that. Whether intentionally or not, we go back and forth: we face fear and loss and then produce in order to overcome it. And then, in an environment of stability, in which fear has been limited, we see production slow or even stop. We fall back into war. We seesaw back and forth.

The most successful of our societies embrace a middle road. But we don't seem to get beyond that.

This book is about getting beyond that. This book is about enabling what the great John Wilberforce called Industry *and* Charity. It is about building systems that enable everyone to step onto the road of fulfillment while leaving no one saddled by fears we can successfully mitigate. It is about enabling people to live the best lives they can live.

While I came to this approach from a religious perspective, you don't have to. The benefits of fulfillment are well understood outside of a religious framework. And so are the costs of fear.

My challenge to you is this: My imaginary Candidate Everyone is full of ideas, but they are ideas almost nobody shares. While there is also a lot more depth (and breadth) to these ideas than what is included in the book, none of them are actually realistic. Just like the book, they are a vague fantasy. The fact is the bridge to realism requires a few things I don't have. Things like real political and bureaucratic expertise, in-depth knowledge of political structures, personal experience of the division of responsibilities between government entities and, of course, a whole lot of important friends.

In order to help build this bridge, I've bought a website. You guessed it: CandidateEveryone.com. As of this writing, there is nothing on there. But I want to use it to work over the policies, improving and strengthening them. I want to use it to lay out how they could exist, not only in the United States but in other countries. Finally, I want to use the site to coordinate actual efforts to bring these sorts of ideas to life.

And I want to invite *you* to take part.

Whether you're an ordinary woman in a tract home, a planner, a politician, a house husband or *whatever*, I'd like you to help build a community.

The community of Candidate Everyone.

You can start by sharing *this* book. Review it on Amazon, tell your friends about it, and recommend it to any reviewers you might now. But then, go a step further and sign up on CandidateEveryone.com.

Together we can use our talents to build a better world.

About the Author

Joseph Cox lives in Modiin, Israel and is blessed with a wonderful wife and six children.

That's me!

Other Books by the Author

Adult Fiction

The City on the Heights (a novel)

Medicine, Torah Shorts Volume 1

The Boulevard, Torah Shorts Volume 2

The Assessors, Torah Shorts Volume 3

Pete and the Felon, Torah Shorts Volume 4

The Barn, Torah Shorts Volume 5

The Hidden Agent (not yet published, learn more at josephcox.com)

Children's Fiction

Grobar and the Mind Control Potion

Squiggles and the Pit of Destruction

www.ingramcontent.com/pod-product-compliance
Lightning Source LLC
Chambersburg PA
CBHW021201130626
46554CB00005B/1919